MW00990221

JEEP TOUR

Jeep Tour

A Novel

GAIL WARD OLMSTED

Jeep Tour
by Gail Ward Olmsted

Cover design by Tugboat Design
Published by Jericho Road Press

This is a work of fiction. Names, characters, places, brands, media, and incidents are either the product of the author's imagination or are used fictitiously. Any resemblance to similarly named places or to persons living or deceased is unintentional.

PRINT ISBN: 978-0-6927-0674-9
LOC: 2015911153

To my husband Deane—my best friend and favorite person in the world. You are the only one I could ever imagine taking this crazy life journey with. Thank you for being so supportive of me and for loving me so well!

To my mom—Anne Brennan Ward. You have taught me the power of unconditional love. No one is sweeter or kinder than you.

To my children—Hayley, my smart and sassy daughter, and Conor, my wise and witty son. I love you both more than you can possibly know.

And in memoriam—my cousin and first best friend, Kathy Ward Barry. The bravest, most amazing woman I have ever known. Hey Kath—love you more!!

Preface

If you ever get the chance for a do-over, take it. That's the best advice I can offer you. Life is rarely predictable, so if the ball is in your court, take it and run with it. How I got where I am today is a pretty good example. A series of random occurrences followed by a single conscious act on my part. And here I am!

Out of all the conferences I could have attended last year, I chose one held in Phoenix. Out of all the touristy activities available, we chose a Jeep tour of the desert. Does fate play a role? If one of us had asked for a third cup of coffee at breakfast or dawdled in just one more gift shop that morning, would we have been assigned to a different tour guide? Is it all about the luck of the draw? If so, is that a good thing?

I have been studying and teaching consumer behavior for most of my adult life and if I've learned one thing in all those years, it would have to be that consumer behavior is influenced by emotion and therefore it's unpredictable and, from an objective third party point of view, often makes no sense.

I guess that's true for *all* behavior, not just in the marketplace. I can't look you in the eye and tell you that everything I've done over the past year or so has been rational.

It certainly wasn't predictable, not based on my first 39 years. Honestly, it could even be viewed as crazy. But I was *not* an objective third party, *not* a casual observer. I was totally committed, in deep, up to my eyeballs actually. Life got messy and scary and then kind of sad ... until it wasn't. At the time, every decision I made and every step I took seemed reasonable, and when I consider where I am today, I honestly wouldn't change a thing. Not a single thing!

CHAPTER 1

Twelve Months Earlier

"Need a hand?" Our tour guide was speaking to me, as I was the last one to board the brightly colored Jeep. "Yes, thanks," I mumbled as he took my hand and helped me into the open back seat.

"You dropped this," he told me as he handed me my water bottle. Glistening with condensation, it slipped from my hand a second time and rolled under the Jeep.

"Sorry," I apologized when he bent down to retrieve it. When he stood upright, I really saw him for the first time.

I gave a small gasp. God, he was gorgeous. Tall, built, and tan, with a shock of blond streaked hair and dazzling green eyes.

"It's okay," he said. "I always end up crawling around under the Jeep for one thing or another." X-rated images of him crawling around on me flashed before my eyes, but I quickly dismissed them. I'm a middle-aged tourist, not some sex-starved guide groupie. But could I be both?

'Don't be ridiculous,' I told myself. Obviously, my lustful thoughts were not reciprocated. Mr. Hunk patted my hand rather absentmindedly, and swung himself into the driver's seat. He turned the key and the Jeep roared to life.

"OK then, ladies … before we set off today, I'd like to introduce myself, find out a little about you, and go over a few ground rules. I'm Rick and I'll be your tour guide. Have any of you been on a tour of the desert before?" I looked over at the other two inhabitants of the Jeep, my colleagues Kate and Linda. Linda spoke for the three of us, since she was riding shotgun, and since she was Linda.

"No, we haven't. You're our first, Rick," she replied. *Oh grief, was she flirting with him?* We've been there before, Linda and I. She gets this southern-fried thing going on and although she's never lived further south than Rhode Island, it somehow works for her. But it's wrong on so many levels.

'Not now, Linda,' I begged silently.

"So Rick, is this *really* the best tour in all of Arizona?" she drawled.

"Why yes, ma'am," Rick replied. "You ladies have come to the right place." He beamed at Linda, who smiled back at him like they were sharing a secret. Leave it to Linda. She always spoke up first, always got noticed, and always took center stage.

"I'm Linda," she said as she extended her hand to Rick.

"Well, hello there. And who are your friends, Linda?" he responded, still grasping her hand.

"That's Kate and her camera, and this is Jax," said Linda pointing to me.

"Hi, Jack," said Rick shaking my hand, before turning to Kate.

"It's Jax," I corrected him.

"What?" said Rick turning back towards me.

"It's Jax," I murmured. "Not Jack."

"Jax?" he questioned. Knowing I should just shut up, I found myself explaining how I had been named after former

First Lady Jacqueline Kennedy. What can I say? My Irish-American parents came of age in the 60's. But as a toddler, I lisped and referred to myself as 'Jackth' and the name stuck. "But you can call me Jackie," I finished rather inanely. Sensing my discomfort, Linda chimed in "and you can call me Linda," and then she started chattering away about how we had been attending an academic conference in Phoenix, and had decided to visit Sedona for some R & R and a quick overnight visit. Rick listened patiently as Linda told him that all three of us were faculty members at a small private college in New England: Linda in Accounting and Finance, Kate in Management Studies, and me in Marketing. At that, Rick turned and looked at me.

"Marketing? I took a class in Marketing. I remember the four P's." I smiled.

"Yeah, I get that a lot," I said. "But it's really more about ..."

"OK, ladies, we're off," Rick interrupted. "I'll go over the ground rules on our way to the desert." Rick drove through the lot and turned right onto the busy surface road. As he wove his way through the heavy midday Sedona traffic, he began explaining some of the sights that we would be seeing. I vaguely remember him talking about keeping our arms inside the Jeep and how we should stay belted in. Something about the need to drink lots of water and that he had a cooler with plenty of cold bottles. He may have said more, but I honestly don't remember. What he was saying was pretty inconsequential. I was still blown away by how good-looking he was. Shallow, I know. He could have been reading from a phone book for all I cared. From my current vantage point, I could only see the back of his head, the gold-streaked hair that grazed the collar of his khaki tour guide shirt, and his massive tanned right forearm as it maneuvered the steering wheel. *Yikes.* I couldn't see his left hand and I wondered if he wore a ring. *Hmmm.* Confident that I had seen all I could for now, I started to pay attention, to listen to him. He spoke clearly and it was pretty easy to hear him over the road noise and the midday traffic. I struggled to place the slight accent that I detected. I am an amateur linguist and I have a knack for identifying where someone might have grown up. But I also know that it's not always accents that identify your place of birth; sometimes it's the words themselves or the phrasing. For instance, if someone says their hair needs washed or their pants need pressed, you can just about guarantee that they were raised in the Pittsburgh area. It's true. But I digress. Struggling to focus, I heard Rick ask Kate about her camera and promise her some amazing shots that afternoon.

"This really is the best tour," he boasted. "Everyone loves it."

"How long have you been giving Jeep tours, Rick?" Linda asked, accent-free.

"Almost three years," he replied. "I came here on vacation and fell in love with the blue skies and red rocks. Went back, quit my job, and here I am."

"Where?" I piped in.

"Where?" asked Rick hesitantly without turning around.

"I mean, where are you from?" I added.

"All around," Rick replied casually. "I went to college for a couple of years in Pennsylvania and lived in Ohio for a while.

I worked as a computer tech, but I was miserable working in a little cubicle. I love it out here in the desert. I can't imagine ever leaving. Okay, we're going off road here, so hang on. This is where the pavement ends and the adventure begins."

Over the next hour or so, Rick showed us the sights. We traveled up steep inclines and down narrow trails. We bounced over an old wagon road that used to be a cattle trail. I loved how enthusiastic he was about everything, how he seemed to delight in all the beauty and unique qualities of the desert. Also, he was very knowledgeable—he really knew what he was talking about. Rick identified the unofficial state flower—the prickly pear cactus.

"It's edible and is used in so many different things. You should try the prickly pear jelly. We can barely keep it in stock in the gift shop," he assured us.

"Hmmm. Sounds nummy," Linda purred. *Honestly.*

At one point, we got out to stretch our legs, and Linda and Kate hurried off to take more pictures. Actually, Kate was taking the pictures that Linda was telling her to take, but whatever their dynamic, it allowed me to get to know Rick a little more. Just a little bit. Rick was a better listener than a talker, so I ended up doing most of the talking. They say nature abhors a vacuum. Well, so do I. At even a hint of a potentially awkward silence, you can count on me to jump in to save the day. I told him about how I was up for tenure and that the decision would be announced any day now. I may have flirted a bit in my rather awkward yet endearing manner. I may have hinted that as a college professor, I had summers off. I may have even suggested that I had access to a boatload of frequent flyer miles. I was trying to subtly communicate my potential availability without being too forward. Hey, use what you've got, right? To be truthful, those miles had been racked up by my jet-setting ex, but I'm pretty certain that I had some coming to me as part of last year's divorce settlement. So, I talked and Rick smiled and looked thoughtful and said things like "Is that right?" at all the appropriate moments.

A little while later, we left the mesa, somewhat reluctantly as the views were stunning for miles, but Rick assured us that there was plenty more to see. I was becoming more comfortable around him and hopefully more appealing as the afternoon wore on. He was receptive to my chatter and we really seemed to hit it off. Linda and Kate had already clambered back into the Jeep and I saw that Linda had relinquished her seat up front to me. I was thrilled to be that much closer to our engaging tour guide. And the amazing vistas. And the tour guide.

"C'mon Jackie, we've got places to go and rocks to see." Rick called out.

"OK, Rick. I'm coming," I responded with probably a bit too much enthusiasm. I could get used to agreeing with him, if you know what I mean. He waited for me and took my arm to help me into my new seat upfront. It was like a date. OK, so *not* a date but I felt a tingle, a really strong reaction to his touch. I think he felt it too. He smiled at me and … wait, was that a wink? Was dating a tourist allowed or was it frowned upon by the official tour guide conduct code? And if allowed, how and when would we manage it? And if not allowed, would he be willing to sneak around or even give up his job for me?

'Hold on, hot stuff,' I cautioned myself. 'Don't get ahead of yourself. He's just flirting to get a bigger tip,' I reasoned. *But still.*

The second half of the tour was even more thrilling. In between explaining why canyons exist (apparently rivers cause erosion—who knew?) and identifying scrub live oak and mistletoe, Rick shared bits of his life with me. Okay, with us, but honestly, I was the only one paying attention. Rapt attention. I learned that he lived alone in a cabin in the woods, loved hiking, was a vegetarian, and that he had been working down in southern Arizona when he first visited Sedona.

"Where in Arizona?" I asked. I'm in marketing and curiosity comes with the territory. It's an occupational hazard, as it were.

"Winslow," he replied. My face brightened. *Winslow, Arizona?* I couldn't help it. I began to hum a line from that Eagles song, *Take it Easy* and was glad when Rick joined in. We hummed a line or two and then sang the last words, ending with a flourish.

"You two make quite a pair. You should consider a lounge act," Linda called from the back of the Jeep.

"Thank you, thank you. We're here all week," I responded. Ignoring Linda, Rick turned to me.

"Yeah," he said, gazing at me appreciatively. "Such a *fine* sight to see."

I blushed and almost dropped my water bottle again. I gulped down a large swallow, before I managed something like, "Oh I bet you say that …" when he reached across the Jeep and wiped a drop of water from my chin.

"No, actually, I never say that," he admitted candidly. *What?* Our eyes met just for a moment and I knew that what I had been feeling wasn't just in my mind or my other body parts. The attraction was mutual. We had chemistry and it was the good kind. We were off again and Rick was deep into a lecture about tectonic plates, before my breathing returned to normal. It had been a while since I had felt such a strong reaction to anyone. Since splitting up with my husband, there hadn't been anyone else of note, not until now.

"Hang on, ladies," Rick called out and I looked up just in time to see a guy in a four-wheeler barreling towards us. Rick expertly turned us out of danger and muttered "Effin' rental" under his breath. "These guys come up here and think that they can handle these vehicles. Like it's a game or something," he complained. Linda leaned forward. Had she been listening the whole time? When she winked at me, I knew that she had been.

"How much training do you need to handle one of these babies?" she asked. Rick explained about the process of becoming a tour guide. He really seemed to take it seriously. He ended with how you weren't able to take a tour out on your own until you had passed all kinds of on and off-road tests.

"What about the rest of it?" I asked.

"The rest of it?" Rick was confused.

"I mean, you know, all the soft skills. The people skills, the knowledge of the desert, and what guests would be seeing."

"Oh, yeah sure," Rick smiled. "Being outgoing helps. You gotta be a people person. They look for someone with some life experience. Someone who has been around a bit. Seen things. Done things. Anywhere else, my resume would be a liability. But not here. And of course, there's classroom training too, and lots of books."

"That would be right up our alley," Linda assured him. "We love being in the classroom, especially Jackie. She's a *really* good teacher." I colored at the sound of my name.

Rick looked at me again and said in a voice that was only meant for my ears, "I bet you would be good at *anything* you put your mind to, Jackie."

In spite of the blazing mid-afternoon sun, I shivered. This really was the best tour ever.

"Oh yeah, you too," I responded. Have we established yet that I'm just a bit of a novice when it comes to flirting?

I never got the knack. It would actually be kind of funny, if it were not so pathetic.

Rick turned our attention back to the path that lay ahead of us. The last hour of the tour was relatively uneventful, I guess, if you call watercolor vistas and harrowing descents uneventful. We drove back through the surface streets towards the tour office and were about to turn into the parking lot when Rick spoke up again.

"How long are you in town?" he asked.

"We're not," I told him apologetically. "We drove down last night and spent the morning shopping and then here. We're heading back to Phoenix now and flying home tomorrow." Rick actually looked disappointed.

"I've got another tour in a little while but, maybe …"

I didn't get to hear whatever "maybe" might entail, because Kate broke in.

"Another tour? Wow, no rest for the weary, huh?" *Great timing, Kate.* Rick told us how three or four tours a day was standard 'in season.' After we pulled into the lot crowded with Jeeps and started to unbuckle our seatbelts, Linda piped up again.

"Can you request a certain guide? Is that possible?" Linda asked with more than a little flirt in her tone.

"Oh yeah, we get that a lot," Rick nodded.

"I bet you do," Linda chuckled and discretely handed him some cash (I later found out it was $50) and promised "Well, if I ever come back to Sedona …" Tour duties over, Rick got busy in his role of consummate company professional and he handed her one of his cards.

"I hope you ask for me. And please, tell your friends. If you want to fill out a quick survey on our website, that'd be great."

"Terrific, thanks again, Rick," Linda concluded, just as Kate went in for a hug. Everyone loves Kate and she gets and gives a lot of hugs. She looked so tiny next to Rick and

I think she caught him a bit off-guard but he recovered quickly and hugged her back. I have never been so jealous of anyone in my life, not since my best friends all went bra shopping back in seventh grade but didn't think to invite me, citing my apparent lack of need at the time. Not much has changed, but I wished right then that I too could pull off a hug. But, no. Sadly, physical displays of affection are just not in my skill set. I would have to settle for a handshake or something equally lame. Note to self: learn to flirt and learn to hug. Basic survival skills especially for the newly single. But for now, the tour had ended. It was time to go and my traveling companions appeared ready to depart.

"Hold on a second, Jackie." Rick disappeared around the counter. He returned just seconds later and handed me a card as well. "Hey, I really enjoyed meeting you. Have a good trip back East. And really, if you're ever out this way …"

"I'll look you up." I assured him. Would I? *Boy, would I.*

He grasped my hand in farewell and I thought he might be leaning in for a hug or something when Kate grabbed my other arm.

"C'mon, Jax. Traffic is gonna be a bear." Vowing revenge on perky Kate and all of her well-intentioned but poorly timed interruptions, I turned to wave at Rick and he smiled back at me.

"Take care," I called out "and thank you." He waved and then turned and disappeared through an open doorway into what looked like a break room of some sort. *Sigh.* Oh well, it was fun while it lasted.

Linda and Kate were already walking towards the parking lot. I hurried along to catch up, but I was too late. Kate was already in the driver's seat and Linda had claimed the front seat of our tiny rental car by the time I reached them.

I was going to be squished in the back with my knees up around my ears for the two-hour ride back to Phoenix. But somehow, I didn't care all that much. The warm glow I was feeling had nothing to do with the temperature. As I struggled to make room for my long legs in a backseat designed for a toddler, I looked at the business card he had handed me. Listed beneath a brightly colored logo was Rick Bowers, *Professional Tour Guide*. The office number and website address were listed as well. When I turned the card over, I gasped. There were the digits that would change my life. He had written in a cramped hand what could only be his cell phone number, with a note. 'Call me,' it read.

CHAPTER 2

Whack-a-Mole

I subscribe to the Whack-a-Mole theory of life. I'm pretty sure it's a philosophy that I invented and it makes a lot of sense. Let me explain. First off, you know Whack-a-Mole, right? That carnival game where a player is issued a large mallet and is instructed to bash the heads of the little mole figures that keep popping up from their holes? The order is random, as is the timing. You might get two to three pop-ups in quick succession, followed by a relatively calm moment with only one at a time. Okay, stay with me here. Those moles? They represent what happens in our lives. Think about it. You finally get over your breakup? Ready to date again? BAM—pink slip at work. You finally find a new job and BAM—your sister calls to announce she's pregnant by her married boyfriend. The baby's born healthy and BAM—your landlord announces that your building is going condo and you don't have the down payment. See what I mean? A series of unrelated and seemingly random events that can singularly cause stress and anxiety and collectively lead you to ponder the age-old questions: "Why me?" "What's next?" or as American wit Dorothy Parker so elegantly asked: "What fresh hell is this?"

I have proof. A friend of mine has suffered from migraines since her teens. Truly debilitating headaches that completely overwhelmed her for two or three days a time. Well, she got pregnant and for nine months she was nauseous and vomited several times a day. Couldn't keep much food down. Wasn't gaining enough weight. I would visit her and bring extra thick chocolate milkshakes. Of course, I would order one for myself, too. I'm a friend, not a saint. And no one likes to drink alone. But my point is that for nine months, Sarah experienced 24-hour morning sickness, but never a single migraine. Not even a tension headache, nothing. She had a healthy baby girl, carried her full term and everything. Nursed her around the clock for about ten weeks. Totally sleep deprived, but happy in a way I had never seen her before. But as soon as she stopped breast-feeding? BAM—migraines returned with a vengeance. Her daughter is now in middle school and Sarah still gets migraines. Why did they disappear for almost a year and then return? Her doctor cited hormones or some scientific nonsense that seemed to make sense to Sarah. Not me. It's Whack-a-Mole. You never get more crap than you can actually handle, but it can be overwhelming at times and you never know what's around the corner. As soon as one situation or problem is resolved, another one pops up. Whack-a-Mole! Think about it. Makes sense, right? I'm not a defeatist. Not a half empty glass kind of person (the glass is just too big—everyone knows that). My dad died, my mom died, I got a divorce. All big things. Shitty things. Things that cumulatively would have knocked me out. But they didn't happen all at once. Except for both my parents dying within a few months of each other. But in between, good things. Plenty of them. Meeting Robbie. Marrying him. Buying a great house. Getting a good job. Robbie's promotion. See what I mean? Breathing moments that allow you to build up your strength for the next mole. I approach each day with enthusiasm and eagerly *carpe diem* my way through life. Really, I do. But I remain ever vigilant for that next mole, that next seemingly random occurrence or problem or situation or whatever. They're designed to throw you off your game, challenge your equilibrium, and test your resolve. But in the game of life, you don't get a huge furry stuffed animal as a prize for whacking the most moles. No. You just get to keep your mallet, ready to swing it for another day. Game over? No, not an option. Keep watching. Keep swinging.

CHAPTER 3

♫ Blowin' in the Wind ♫

"Your sunglasses? Ma'am, your sunglasses."

"Huh?"

"Ma'am, you need to remove your sunglasses," the TSA agent spoke with an intensity that I found just a bit intimidating. 'Airport personnel are just so darn cheery', said no traveler ever.

"Oh, sorry," I pushed my sunglasses up over my forehead.

"Jax, what's with you?" Linda hissed at me. "It's like you're out of it." I had no response to that. I *was* out of it.

Making sure that the face I presented matched the one on my driver's license, the agent looked carefully at me. What did he see, I wondered? I was a quickly approaching-forty-year-old academic, disheveled from rushing to get to the airport for our early morning flight. The drive from Sedona last night had taken us longer than we had planned, and after a dinner of appetizers and margaritas at the hotel bar, I collapsed into a restless sleep. I had felt fuzzy and disoriented ever since my crack of dawn wakeup call, despite gulping down a large coffee on the way to the airport. An early morning flight had seemed like a good idea when we had made our plans last month. I could only hope to get in some sleep on the flight home in order to be standing upright the next day, which I knew would be full of classes and a department meeting to boot. Call me a lightweight, but I do better with eight hours of sleep in my own bed and a diet of three squares a day and a lot less booze.

Did the uniformed agent see the network of crow's feet just starting to make their appearance? The under-eye circles that no amount of night cream would fade? On the plus side, I had thick reddish-brown hair that had not yet begun to go gray, green eyes, a sprinkling of freckles on my nose, a high forehead and a wide mouth. Cover girl? Not hardly. But, not bad. Good enough. The same face or close to it that I had been staring at in the mirror for my whole life. I used to give myself little pep talks as I prepared to leave home each morning. I would smile broadly at the young girl/young woman/not-so-young woman in the mirror, nod encouragingly, and say something like 'looking good' or 'go get 'em tiger' or 'you go, girl' or occasionally, 'what the hell are you looking at?'

Done with me and seemingly satisfied that I was who I claimed to be, the agent handed my license back to me and called the next victim, er, passenger. I walked through the scanner without incident and then stopped at the nearest bench to put on my shoes (slip on, natch), grab my cardigan sweater (it gets chilly in airports), and organize my handbag and carryon. I double-checked, making sure that I could locate my boarding pass. I have been known to misplace a movie ticket in the short time it takes to walk over to the ticket taker. I have a lot on my mind, okay? Linda and Kate were waiting, so we hustled over to grab a bite to eat before they called our flights.

After a simply delightful breakfast containing not a single item from any of the major food groups (but it is the most important meal of the day, and my personal favorite) during which we stood toe-to-toe with our fellow travelers and Linda swears she was groped, we split up. I had only been approved to attend the conference a few weeks back, long after Linda and Kate had booked their flights. The return flight that they had chosen was full, so I had booked a more expensive direct flight home and was going to pay the difference out of pocket. Kate and Linda had to make a connection in Chicago and despite leaving sooner than I did, they would get in two hours later.

I relished the idea of being alone for the next several hours. I was tired of talking and compromising—where and when to eat, which radio stations to listen to in the car. I looked forward to being alone. I wanted time with my thoughts. A secret smile lit up my face. Rick. God, he was cute. No, not cute, Robbie, my ex, was cute. Rick was bigger, more rugged. Devastatingly gorgeous? Yes. *Not* cute.

When my flight was finally called, I settled in to my comfy business class seat and gratefully accepted the bottled water that the attendant offered. The seat next to me stayed vacant so I got cozy with my pillow and my Kindle. And my thoughts-of blue skies, red rocks, and strong hands covering mine. Those green eyes were hard to forget. As was that killer smile.

Hours later, my fellow passengers and I landed. No clue as to why, but we rushed like mad to the carousel assigned to our flight and began the wait. Waiting for your luggage is like waiting to get picked for a team in grade school gym class. Think about it. You want to get chosen, but while waiting, you start to feel a certain camaraderie with the others. As your classmates/fellow travelers get chosen before you, you start to panic. *What if I'm last or don't get picked at all?*

As soon as your name is called or your luggage appears, you have nothing in common any longer with the rest of the group. You're relieved, proud, happy. Without feeling a twinge of guilt, you skip forward, join your team, and never look back. Triumphant, victorious, a winner. I remembered feeling this way in gym class. Those of us waiting to be called suffered silently. 'Pick me, pick me,' your inner voice begged. Shame and fear had brought us together. We're like our own sad little team. Wait, was that my name? Was that me they were pointing at? Yes, yes it was—see you losers later. I'm outta here.

So for now, it was hurry up and wait. I recognized that black bag. I've seen it several times by now. Its owner had the forethought to tie a jaunty pink polka dot bow on it. To make it stand out, I guessed. But where was she? I assumed the owner was a female, but you never know, do you? At any rate, the bag continued on its lonely circuitous route, while those of us still waiting grew increasingly concerned about the alarming lack of new luggage on the carousel. I'd worried that my bag wouldn't make it, even before I had boarded my flight. Something about the way the baggage attendant didn't make eye contact or even respond to my forced but cheery greeting many hours ago. It was a sign. I doubted that my bag and I would be reunited this evening. The next time I laid eyes on it would be when I stumbled downstairs after being awakened by a doorbell-ringing taxi driver sometime in the middle of the night. Would I need to tip him and if so, how much? I mean it wasn't *his* fault. But it wasn't my fault either. This is the kind of thing that I obsess about way too often.

I watched my fellow passengers jostle their way towards the carousel whenever fresh luggage made its debut. Some were more aggressive. They had seen their bag and were going to claim it, damn it. Others were tentative, less certain. Was that my black/navy/grey 26-inch Pullman or not? Need to get closer for a better look. No, not mine. Disappointment clouded their features as they stepped back to let others move forward. Out of the corner of my eye, I saw the mud brown, slightly scuffed suitcase that was part of a five-piece set I'd purchased years ago at a wholesale club.

It was mine "Excuse me- that's my bag," I declared loudly with pride. Mr. Baggage Attendant had done his job after all. I would sleep undisturbed tonight. No doorbell jarring my sleep during my first night back at home.

I pushed my way through the crowd, grabbed my bag and took off for the exit, three of the four wheels humming along. The cold night air was refreshing after breathing in stale airplane fumes all day. While I searched for signs of the shuttle that would take me to the parking lot, I regretted my decision to cheap out and not spring for valet parking. I realized my car would be coated with ice and with no guarantee of starting on the first try. It was just a few minutes later, while I was riding the noisy overheated shuttle, that I first heard the voice. 'Sell it, donate it, get rid of it. Buy something new and drive it to Sedona' it said. What? No way. I couldn't think like that. But apparently, I could. That particular train of thought chugged along, picked up steam and would not be stopped by mere reason or logic. I wondered how much I could get for it? My car, I mean. I'd be selling it, I'm sure, along with many of my worldly possessions in order to make a fresh start in Arizona. Was I serious? Was I ready to make some changes? All for that smile and those hands attached to those forearms? *Yikes.* Give up my apartment and my job, say goodbye to my friends and move to the Southwest? No more freezing winters, no more grading papers and no more department meetings. But I love my job, don't I? And I'm about to be granted tenure.

I debated calling the number that Rick had given me. Was it his home? His cell? Was this some sort of cruel joke where he would have given me a phony number? But why would he do that? He didn't strike me as someone who could be intentionally mean. And if I did reach him, what would I say? 'Hi, it's me. Jackie. Just wanted to let you know that I made it home, safe and sound.' *Ugh*. No, I would need a plan. Better sleep on this.

After stowing my bag in the trunk, I started my car. I hopped back out and hunkered down to scrape at the thick glaze of ice on my windshield with my fingers, deciding that travel was overrated and a huge pain in the ass. But my car had started right up, despite five days in freezing weather. Was that a sign? And, if so, of what?

"First time, every time," I murmured aloud and mentally added $500 to the selling price.

After paying a small fortune to the parking lot attendant and pocketing the crumpled receipt, I headed north. Back home. As I drove through the dark but familiar streets, I kept thinking to myself, could I really do this? Just pick up and leave everything that I know, everyone that I know? Well, why not? I live here because my parents had lived here. I had stayed local for college and graduate school, for my first job and for my current job. It was time. My time, time to leave the nest. What was here that was so important? Friends? Sure. A job? Yeah. But no real family. Robbie, my ex. My apartment. My chiropractor. The thought that had been welling up inside of me for the past twenty-four hours started to take over. 'Move,' it said. 'Head west. Pack up and move to Arizona.'

"And do what?" my practical self responded. Give up a great job, tenure and security for a painted desert, a pair of green eyes, and a set of abs that I imagined wouldn't quit. I could sell my car, store my stuff, take a sabbatical, forward my mail. Why not? It's not like I needed to get a new job right away. I could live off my savings for a while if I had to. But that money is saved for later, some day, when I really need it.

'You *really* need this,' that voice whispered.

Home at last, I sorted through the stack of mail that had accumulated during the last several days and opened the fridge. I was contemplating brewing a pot of coffee when the phone rang. It was Susan, my best friend.

"Hi, you made it home. Everything good?"

"Yes, fine," I replied. "Thanks for bringing in my mail."

"Oh, no problem," said Suze. "How was it?"

"Oh good, the conference was a little long, but Sedona was lovely."

"I knew you would enjoy it. I want to hear more." But when I failed to respond, she added, "but I'll let you go. Talk soon." I love that about Suze. She knew when to fold 'em.

I hung up and decided to make some tea instead. Herbal, as I planned to sleep at some point tonight. I was getting out a mug when the phone rang again. I assumed it was Suze wanting to share some local gossip that just wouldn't wait until the morning.

"What did you forget?" I answered teasingly.

"Jaxie, it's me."

"Robbie?"

"Yeah, who were you expecting?"

"Oh just Suze, you know, girl talk. What's up?"

"I thought you were going to call me when you got back?"

"I just now walked in the door," I protested. Defensive, why was I defensive?

"Want me to come over?"

"Now?" My voice cracked. Really, it cracked. "No, it's late, I have to unpack and shower and get some sleep and it's a ..."

"School night," Robbie finished for me. "Okay, rain check?" I agreed to call him the next day and hung up the phone. Why did I feel so guilty? I hadn't done anything wrong. Yet.

I nixed the tea, stripped down and pulling an old t-shirt over me, slipped into bed. Cold sheets and warm thoughts. *Could I do this?* Thoughts of the desert and Rick's face and his green eyes and blond streaked hair were the last things I remembered before I fell asleep. I was home, for now.

CHAPTER 4

♫ Running on Empty ♫

After a day spent traveling, you'd think I would be primed for a deep, sound sleep back in my own bed. But instead, I spent the night turning and tossing. Turning the idea of changing my life over in my mind and tossing it back out. Over and over. You can do this. No, it's crazy. I pictured walking into work and asking for a sabbatical. But I should probably wait 'til I got tenure, right? The decision was due any day now. Everyone on the tenure committee told me I was a shoe-in. So how long after getting tenure would I be eligible for a sabbatical? And what exactly is a sabbatical, anyhow, and how does it differ from a paid vacation? What could I get for my car? How much would it cost to ship all my stuff? Or should I just start over? It had always been a fantasy of mine. No more fraying towels and faded sheets. No more mismatched plates. It was hard to throw things out when they still worked, were still functional. But everything new and fresh? *I know, what a thrilling fantasy right?* But hey, I teach consumer behavior, give me a break. It's not like I couldn't afford it. I was ready for a rainy day. Or maybe a blue sky, red rock sunny one? Around dawn, I finally fell into a deep sleep. I can't prove it, but I'm pretty sure I was smiling.

The next morning, I showered, made coffee, thawed a hunk of coffee cake (homemade, my specialty), dressed in my uniform and headed out to my car. I don't really wear a uniform. It's just that I have a closetful of mix and match separates, primarily dark trousers, colorful shells and blouses, and an array of neutral cardigans and jackets. And low-heeled shoes. Makes getting dressed a snap. Boring, but easy. That would describe my style. Especially for work. For dressy nights, I had a trio of knit sheath-type dresses that skimmed the tops of my knees. A sleeveless black one, a three-quarter-sleeved floral number and a cap sleeved one in teal—I was ready for just about everything.

When my car started right up again, despite the cold, I mentally added another yet $500 to the selling price. *Oh stop it. Grow up.* I drove to work blaring oldies on the radio. *Walking on Sunshine* was the only song I remembered during my short commute. And I was.

I found a spot close to the walkway. Had to be a good omen. It was great to be back. I said "hello" to half a dozen students as I crossed the campus to the brick and ivy building that housed the School of Business. Home, yes, I was home. After seven years of full-time employment and a couple of years of adjunct work before that, it was the longest I had ever spent working in one place. I loved my job and my co-workers. I wished I had made good on my thoughts of bringing back some Southwestern goodies. Maybe some of that jelly Rick was so fond of? I could have left some tasty snacks in the break room with a note. "From Sedona—Enjoy- Jax." But like many of my good intentions, the follow up was lacking. I had lots of great ideas, but honestly? I acted on very few of them.

I took the stairs two at a time and greeted the receptionist cheerfully.

"Hey, Ellen."

"Hi Jackie," she said, sounding reserved and maybe a little pissed off. Now I really wished I had brought something back, maybe even a small cactus for her desk. Crap, I thought. I should have…

"Jackie," Ellen interrupted my litany of shoulddas. "He wants to see you." He, of course referred to Bill, our boss. Dean of the School of Business.

"Right now?" I squeaked. "I need to prep for class and …"

"Now, Jackie," she said, a little sadly or so it seemed. *Weird.* "You can go right in." WTF? Maybe he just wanted to get an idea of what his generosity in sending me to the conference had yielded. What had I learned that I could bring into the classroom? Shit, I couldn't think of a thing. Except that sun and those hands. *Stop it.* I crossed the lobby to Bill's office, knocked once and let myself in.

"Dean," I said, "Hi. I'm back."

"Have a seat, Jackie. Please." He started right in.

No pleasantries. No "How was your flight?" Suddenly, a plush and very expensive Oriental rug was being pulled out from under my feet. *Wait, what?* Patiently, as if he was talking to a somewhat dimwitted freshman on academic probation, I heard the words again, but only a few of them made any sense. Budget cuts, enrollment trends, other departments needing resources. That was always a theme of Bill's. It was his reason for everything. The fierce competition between the various departments of the college. Think win-win? No, not here. If someone else gained, you lost. One department's good fortune was at the expense of another's. Bill used to joke, but not in a humorous way, that the battles over resources on the campus were so bitter because the spoils were so few. Or something like that. It's called Sayre's Law. Google it. Bottom line, I was out at the end of the semester. Done for. Done diddly done for. *Shit.*

"Maybe you can still teach a course or two. Talk to Linda," Bill said, throwing me a bone. As if a part-time adjunct stipend was a prize to be celebrated.

"I have to go. I'm sorry, I've got to go," I stammered. *Sorry? I just said I was sorry?* I got up and walked out, leaving my canvas tote bag on the floor. Passing Ellen at a fast clip, I ran down the steps and out the door. For once the smokers didn't piss me off. They huddled in the cold just feet from the entrance, puffing away. Nation-wide, college campuses were going smoke-free. But not here. On this campus, smokers moved freely among the rest of us all over the outdoor common areas. Today, I ignored them and took in great gulps of cold, nicotine-laced air. I was downsized, terminated. No tenure, no job? What the fuck was I going to do now?

I had never taken my coat off and my keys were still in my pocket. By the time I got to my office, Ellen must have retrieved my belongings from Bill's office and left them for me. Somehow, I made it through the morning, teaching my classes as if on autopilot. I returned to my office a few hours later and lost in thought, jumped when Linda stuck her head in.

"Got time for lunch?" I looked at her carefully. *Was that guilt? Yes.*

"You knew," I accused.

"Wait, Jackie," she protested.

"You knew and you let me go on all week about tenure and all my plans and all the time you knew they were shit-canning me?" To her credit, she didn't deny it.

"What did you want me to do?" she asked. "Ruin our, er, your trip? What good would that have done?"

"You should have told me," I whispered. Linda had earned tenure years ago and as a department chair, she was privy to a lot of the behind-the-scenes maneuverings that defined our world. I looked away. There was nothing more I wanted to say to her right then. Maybe ever. I continued to ignore her and she finally left.

"Call me later," she said. "We can meet for a drink; I'm buying." *Don't hold your breath,* I thought morosely. Oh great, a drink. Combined with the offer to teach part-time, things were really looking up. I was about to launch into a full-scale pity party, party of one, when Kate popped in. I gave her the death glare.

"Don't look at me like that," she begged. "I didn't know, not until this morning. And don't blame Linda. She was in a tough spot."

"Oh yeah, let's feel sorry for Linda. I'm the one out on the street." At least Kate didn't offer alcohol or part-time wages. She knew me better than that. She was more likely to show up at my apartment later in the week with a couple of pints—of ice cream—probably Ben & Jerry's. Even in a tough economy, all but the most cash-strapped of us still opt for the affordable luxuries—manicures, $4 coffees and name brand ice cream.

"I know, Jax. It sucks. It really does. I'm so sorry."

She plodded silently back down the hall and I could hear her turning the key to her office. Which would be a mess. Stacks of papers, graded and ungraded, textbooks, some still in plastic wrap from the publishers and notes from students that had graduated. I love Kate, but she's a hot mess, for sure.

I pulled on my coat and shoved some papers that needed grading in my bag. Time to go home and put an end to this crappy day. Knowing that missing the department meeting would guarantee that my spectacular fall from grace would be #1 on the agenda; I trudged out to the faculty parking lot. It wasn't until I got into my car and started it up that the little voice came back. The one that said, 'Now you can do it; no job to quit. You've got to start over, might as well do it in Sedona.'

With a smile, I pulled out of the parking lot and headed for home. *Maybe I could do this.*

CHAPTER 5

♫ In My Life ♫

My parents hadn't wanted me. Apropos of nothing, right? But before you call a waa-mbulance, let me explain. I was a change of life baby. My mom had just turned forty-one when she found out she was pregnant. Four months along and she thought it was indigestion until a store clerk asked her when she was due. My dad was five years older and they had been married for ten years when I came along. They were accountants, CPAs. Partners with their own firm. They lived together, worked together, commuted together. They finished each other's sentences. They were joined at the hip. Not much room for a baby, let alone a lisping toddler or a pigtailed rope-jumping, question-asking grade-schooler, or a mopey pre-teen with braces and too-long bangs. My dad would sometimes walk into a room and seem surprised to find me there. Not just in that particular room, but in his life. "That's my girl," he'd say, as if trying to convince himself. I learned to be quiet, tried to be good and asked very little of them. I took to reading in the break room at their office afternoons when I got out of school. Once they forgot me. Really, literally locked up, turned out the lights, and drove halfway home before they realized. I had fallen asleep on the carpeted floor and woke up when they came rushing in. My dad tried to stage an *ad hoc* game of hide and seek, but I knew and they knew I knew, so whatever. I didn't take it personally. I mean they hadn't asked for me and never really knew what to do with me. It's not like I was abused or anything. I was an asset but they didn't know where I fit in the balance sheet of their lives. *Yeah, I said it.* As if by some unspoken agreement, they pretty much let me be and I never gave them any trouble. But I know they loved me in their way and I think they were proud of me. In high school, I did everything right. Oh, not that I was super popular or prom queen or anything but I got really good grades, mostly kept my curfew, had a small group of close friends and graduated with honors. I spent a lot of time alone in my room listening to Duran Duran and U2. At sixteen, *Joshua Tree* rocked my world. I had a couple of boyfriends, nothing too serious. You would think that I would've been a perfect candidate to apply to colleges across the country and move out on my own. I could've gotten into just about any school I wanted. Not the ivies maybe, but close. I had the grades and while not über-rich, my parents could have afforded to pay private school tuition. But for whatever reason, it never occurred to me to leave home to go to school. When I announced my plans to commute to the local branch of the state university, my guidance counselor said fine, my parents said fine, and that was it. College seemed like an extension of high school and that was okay. It was fine.

My parents died just months apart (my father of a heart attack and my mother of a broken heart, although doctors cited a blood clot) while I was in my senior year of college. I was devastated and kind of scared. I had loved them and

I missed their steadying influence in my life. I was alone, adrift. Weeks later, I decided to skip the commencement ceremony commemorating yet another ending, and drove by myself to the Cape for a weekend of beach walking, reading, and lobster eating. I was feeling pretty lost. But—a good accountants' daughter—I was practical and I knew what had to be done. Soon after I returned, I sold my folks' share of the practice to two of their partners. Then I packed up their personal belongings and sold their house. I invested all of the money and finally started to think about my own future. I decided that it included a Master's degree in Business Administration. I was way too practical to traipse around Europe for a year and way too chicken to start a business or anything. So back to school for me. I applied and got accepted into the MBA program at the same university I had just graduated from. During this time, I lived in an apartment—three rooms, but all mine. I lived way below my means and saved my money for when I was able to start my life, my real-life. When it would count for something.

By the time I earned my MBA, I knew that I wanted to pursue a career in marketing. Compared to the orderly, black-and-white world of accounting that I had grown up in, advertising and consumer behavior offered something new and exciting to me. I secured an entry-level position at an advertising agency. I found I was a pretty decent writer and developed a good eye for what worked well in ads, especially in print. The clients liked me, trusted me. I traded in my pre-ripped jeans and Converse All-Stars for suits with shoulder pads, silk blouses and dressy black pants. You can never have enough pairs of black pants. Trust me on this. Mostly my boss stuck me on the phones or at the front counter, but while there, I edited a lot of copy and sat in on some of the meetings, both with clients and the creative team. I started dating Josh, one of the copywriters, my first serious adult relationship. All-night sleepovers and everything. They say the past repeats itself and in a weird way, I guess it did. After my divorce, I ended up living in an apartment just down the street from my very first place, and my husband? Yeah, he was an ad guy. But I'm getting ahead of myself. I lasted at the agency for just over two years but after breaking it off with Josh, I was ready to move on.

This time, I chose to go in-house, at a large corporation that had been one of my agency's clients. I know, I need to get out more, right? First job at the same place I had interned and second job working for one of the clients. But wait, there's more. I finally decided to teach and put all of that coursework to good use and you'll never believe where I got hired … no, not the same university where I had spent six years. For that I would have needed a PhD. It was a smaller, private college but in the same town. My MBA and several years of work experience were more than sufficient and I was finally offered a tenure-track instructor-level job at not quite half my salary at the time.

Looking back, I guess that's why people who knew me were so shocked at my decision to relocate to Sedona. It was the first time I had actively sought out a brand-new opportunity for myself. Didn't travel the same old familiar path. I was a lifelong believer in the 'shortest distance between two points is a straight line' axiom. I had followed all the rules and traveled that straight line. Got a degree, a job, got married, bought a house. I thought all that would make me happy, successful. But it hadn't worked out, not for me. I needed to go off-road and find my own way. It was crystal clear to me, at least at the time that this move was my destiny. My future included red rocks and blue skies. Okay, again with the red rocks. But if you go there, you'll see for yourselves. It *is* stunningly beautiful. Honest. Why would I lie?

CHAPTER 6

♫ Into the Mystic ♫

"I think you should do it. It'll be good for you." Those were Robbie's first words when I told him about my plans.

Finally, someone who got it, got me, understood. I should have guessed it would be Robbie. Reactions at work were mixed. My soon-to-be-former colleagues seemed surprised that my decision to leave was as sudden and certain as it was. A few of them even suggested that I stick it out for another year and try for tenure again. The common theme seemed to be 'what do you have to lose?' That didn't seem like an argument to me, at least not a good one. I probably should have fought harder, hell, fought at all. Marched into that cheap bastard Dollar-Bill's office and demand that the decision be overturned. Get students to write letters on my behalf. Request a hearing or a face to face with whoever had decided my fate. But honestly? I'm not a fighter. Not really. I didn't fight to keep my marriage and I wasn't going to fight now. I didn't want to stay where I wasn't wanted. There was no wind left in my sails. I was beginning to feel that the college's decision to not offer tenure was a sign. A sign that it was time to move on, time to pack up and head west.

"You just want to get rid of me," I teased Robbie. "You've been trying to figure out a way to break it off and this is it. This is your chance to do it, once and for all." Although I kept my tone light, down deep his support felt good. His opinion mattered. I trusted him and his instincts. Our marriage hadn't worked out, but there was a deep and long-lasting connection that I knew I would miss. Robbie picked up on it.

"No seriously, Jax, it's a good move for you, you should do it." We were lounging in bed late on a Saturday morning when I broke the news to him. Well, at least part of the news. I neglected to tell him the part about Rick, the part about a crush, and an attraction so powerful that it provided the impetus for me to even consider such a move. So much for full disclosure. And I'm usually 'Queen of the Overshare.' Oh wait; I know what you're thinking. What are you doing in bed with your ex? Oh yeah, that.

The ink was barely dry on our divorce papers when Robbie and I resumed the spectacular physical relationship that had held our seven-year marriage together. We were much better *in* bed than out of it. Honestly, it was magical most of the time. I'm sure that on paper we didn't really make a lot of sense as a couple. But, believe me. We made *a lot* of sense, if you know what I mean. So, it wasn't long after the divorce before we clicked again and everything about it seemed right, except for the goodbyes. Those were still awkward, even after almost two years. I was afraid that Robbie would think that I had nothing better to do but hook up with him, and I didn't want to appear too clingy, too possessive. I was going for hot, yet cool, you know? Available, yet elusive.

It started innocently enough on a Saturday morning, several months after Robbie moved out. We had sold the house and I was organizing things to prepare for my move to an apartment nearby. I left a message for him earlier that week to let him know about my plans. He had left a bunch of things behind, like his golf clubs and some winter clothes, and I needed him to come by to pick them up. So, a few days later, he showed up and made a few trips out to his car. I tried to give him some space and I was sitting on the couch when he was ready to leave. We started out hugging, then cuddling, then tears (mine) led to kissing, then more.

We ended up in bed, and everything was great, until it was time for Robbie to go. I wanted to ask him to stay, because although I'd been alone in the house for the past few months, I knew it would feel really empty again once he left this time. But I didn't ask. I couldn't figure out how. Robbie seemed resigned yet reluctant to leave. With his hands on my shoulders, he peered into my eyes.

"You gonna be okay, Jax?" he asked.

"I'll be fine," I replied. *Don't go.*

"When are you moving?"

"The van will be here next Saturday to pick up the furniture but I'm trying to move my clothes and plants and books during the week. I'll make a lot of trips back and forth." *Don't cry.*

"Do you need any help?" *Yes, I do.*

"No, I should be good. Don't worry about it."

"Maybe I'll come back next Saturday, come to the new place, help you get settled, huh?" Happy at the thought of seeing him again, I could be relaxed, playful.

"Getting settled? Is that what the kids are calling it these days?" I teased. He smiled at me, that special Robbie smile that I've always loved.

"Works for me," he said, kissing the top of my head before he left. I was sitting on the edge of the bed, which made his final act pretty easy. If I had been standing, he would have probably settled on my cheek. I'm tall and he's not that much taller.

I was really busy that week getting ready for final exams (giving them, not taking them) and making the aforementioned trips back and forth from my old house to my new place. "It doesn't really matter whether you're moving a few miles or a few hundred miles," I complained to a coworker. "It's still a pain in the ass."

The thought that kept me going all week was the hope that Robbie would come through for me and show up on Saturday. And he did. Just as the moving truck pulled away from the curb and drove down the street, Robbie was there with flowers, a bottle of wine, a bag of groceries, and Thai takeout. No one had ever looked that good. Romeo in black jeans, baby. Actually, a dark wash blue but you get the picture. After I found something to put the flowers in and stowed away the groceries, mostly staples with all the brands I liked, I gave him a tour of the new place.

"It's not much," I prattled on nervously "but it gets lots of light and it's even closer to the college than our house was." I like to state the obvious whenever possible. Standing in the doorway of the smaller of the two bedrooms, I indicated my plans for my home office. Although the college afforded me an office and shared administrative support, I did a lot of work from home, more so since I'd been on my own. That's one of the really nice perks of working in academia, the ability to work from almost anywhere. Although I preferred to teach the traditional way and avoided online courses, there was still a lot I could do from home: grading, email communication with students, and class prep.

"It's great, Jax, really. I hope you'll be happy here," said Robbie.

"Yeah," I echoed. "It's going to be great." I had treated the moving men to pizza just an hour ago and managed to scarf down a couple of slices myself. But Robbie seemed to want to stay, so I started dishing up the Thai food.

"This looks great," I said "I can't thank you enough." *Great, yeah everything was just great.* The words sounded hollow and insincere. This was Robbie. I reached out to him to squeeze his hand, to let him know how much his being there meant to me. That did it. I think it was the sign that Robbie had been waiting for. He grabbed me and kissed me. I kissed him back. We christened my new place, not once but twice, and ended up eating the Thai food much later. It was the perfect housewarming—so comfortable, so familiar to sit and eat and talk to Robbie at the end of a busy day. But it really hadn't been like that for a while—that comfort, that ease. The last year of our marriage had been punctuated by stress and a reserve between us. Cold, stony silence. Anger, sadness. A fair amount of yelling (him) and lots of tears (me). But hot sex. In spite of all of the dysfunction that had begun to permeate our relationship, great sex was somehow a given. It was like an oasis, a respite from the Sullivan—Colby Cold War.

"See you for dinner?" I'd ask before we both went off to work in the morning those last few months.

"Sure, why not?" Robbie would usually reply. "Did you have plans?"

"No, I mean. Whatever. Should I cook?"

"No, forget it," Robbie would respond. "I'll just pick something up." Game, set, match. I would eat cold cereal on the couch and pretend I didn't notice when he came in hours later than usual. We had started this sick little competition—who could stay away longer? Come home before the other person? You lose. Leave first? You win. Writing a note was a sign of weakness. So was a text message. We never kept score, but I played that game for the last few months of our marriage with a fierceness and competitiveness I had never known I was capable of. It was exhausting and stupid, but we played it right until the bitter end. I think it was a tie.

Tonight, however, the old closeness was there, the friendship and the intimacy that came from all those years together. A small part of me wanted him to stay over, but I was actually glad when he said that he had better get going. Not a good precedent.

"Nine o'clock on a Saturday night," I joked, "what do you have, a hot date?" Hurt clouded Robbie's handsome features.

"No, Jax. It's been a long day and I'm beat."

"I know," I reassured him. "It's fine. I need to find some sheets and start getting settled anyway."

"You'll be great, Jax. You always are." Robbie kissed my cheek and once again, I watched him walk away from me. *Damn.*

I did find those sheets, and towels, and eventually forks and spoons and plates as well. It was kind of exciting getting settled in, being on my own again. I remembered the feelings I had when I moved into my first apartment after college. As a commuter for my undergraduate years, getting my first place after selling my parents' home was a big deal. I had run around purchasing all of the accessories and furnishings for my first apartment. From my parents' home, I brought an ancient sleeper sofa, a coffee table with two matching end tables, and kitchen set with four chairs. And a dresser I had used for at least fifteen years. But the bed was new, queen-sized with nice new sheets and a peaches and cream comforter that I just had to have. I felt so grown-up and so anxious for my life to begin. Fifteen years later, I was at that same point again. I even had the same queen-sized bed. It had been in the guest room of the home that we had purchased just six years earlier. After Robbie moved out, I had taken to sleeping in that bed again. The king-sized bed in the master bedroom just felt so big without him there. I know it sounds cliché, but I just got a better night's sleep in the guest room, night after night.

I got through final exams and continued to get settled in my new place. I'm a nester, it's in my DNA. Even my office at the college. Personal touches and vintage travel posters made it homey, as did the plants that I managed not to kill by taking them home during breaks.

Robbie's Saturday morning visits became regular after our divorce was finalized and once in a while, we would go out to lunch 'after.' Occasionally, we saw a movie or just went for a walk, but most Saturday nights featured a lonely, empty feeling that came over me after Robbie left. I thought about asking him to stop, to keep his distance, to let me move on. But I didn't. I still needed that connection, that time together.

The feeling of being alone didn't last forever and I had recently been making plans with friends and actually keeping them. My single friends were happy to have someone new to play with, and my married friends seemed to delight in inviting me over for family meals or *lovely* dinner parties. But no blind dates. I was really clear about that. I had no interest in meeting that new-to-town college roommate or visiting third cousin. Not now, maybe not ever. I had my work and my friends and my books and my knitting and my DVR. And Robbie in my bed just about every week. I was good, thank you. Just fine.

My best friend Susan didn't get it.

"He's using you, Jax," she would complain to me. She had never been a huge Robbie fan, even as the maid of honor at our wedding nine years earlier.

"Maybe I'm using him," I told her on more than one occasion. "Did you ever think of that?" Yeah, no. She wasn't having it.

"You're kidding yourself if you think that you're really moving on," she said.

"Guys aren't exactly lined up to go out with me," I told her. "It's not like he's keeping me from seeing other people."

"But maybe you'd be more motivated to get out more if you didn't have Robbie to fall back on," she pressed.

"Suze, what do you want from me?" I asked. "It's just how it is. It's just what it is." *Deal with it, ok? And shut up.* Ironically the first words out of her mouth when I told her of my plans to move to Sedona were "What about Robbie?"

"He'll be fine," I told her and I knew he would be. Right? I assumed he had been dating other women during the last couple of years, but I didn't ask. I didn't want to know. But out of all my friends and colleagues that I had told about my plans, Robbie was the only one who didn't hold back. There was no reservation when he hugged me and congratulated me on my decision. No buts or what-abouts?

"What can I do?" he asked. "What do you need?"

The good news was I had enough money to tide me over and Robbie knew it. Not from my meager salary at the college, but in addition to the aforementioned windfalls that had come my way, we had made a healthy profit on our one and only joint real estate transaction. It was the first house either of us had ever owned. It had four bedrooms, a gourmet cook's dream of a kitchen and a large wooded lot. We got it at a good price and sold it six years later for almost double what we paid. Our friends had been skeptical during the search process.

"What do you need four bedrooms for anyway?" they asked. I'm sure some of them even laughed behind our backs at our foolishness and champagne tastes, but we were the ones laughing … all the way to the bank when we sold our home at the height of the market. Even after splitting the money, we were both quite comfortable. It helped to make my decision to move out west -- without even a single contact or hope of a job—a relatively easy one. I could get by for quite a while and still have money to put down on a new home or maybe even a business someday.

"Maybe I'll open a café or a bookstore," I told Suze.

"What about a yarn shop, Jax? You love to knit. You'd be great at it." I looked at her in amazement.

"That's the first positive thing you've said to me about this move," I told her.

"I know, I'm sorry. I just don't love the idea. I'll miss you so much and I hate to see you get your heart broken again."

"The only thing that will break my heart, Suze, is staying here and having to start over again. I need to do this." She threw her arms around me and gave me a big hug.

"I know Jax. You'll be great. Really. I'm glad for you."

"Don't overdo it," I warned. "It's still weeks away." *Plenty of time to change your tune and lay the guilt on nice and thick.* "I've got some wine in the fridge. We can sit out on the porch and chill. C'mon." We had been friends since junior high and I knew I would miss her so much. She had shared my hair scrunchies and given me her 'Michael Jackson in the yellow tux' poster that I coveted. Suze was my rock. Always was.

Throughout my teen years and into adulthood, she was my constant. Steady and supportive. And her family, too. Unlike my home, which was frequently too quiet, hers was teeming with people and activity. Lots of brothers and sisters, very hands-on parents. Arguments. Clutter. Laughter and tears. Lots of hugs. Her mom was always so warm and demonstrative with her affection. When I slept over, she would always tuck us in and pat our cheeks and kiss the tops of our heads.

"Night, night my girls," she would whisper as she turned out the light. And Suze's dad was a trip. He always noticed if our attire was inappropriate for nights out.

"Change your clothes, Susan. And you too, Jackie. No daughters of mine ..." Fill in the blank—jeans too tight, sweaters too low, skirts too short. "And wipe that puss off your face," he would call out as we retreated back to Suze's room to change. Suze would be truly pissed, but honestly? I was thrilled by the attention. My own dad was a dear, but I could have left the house wearing a paper bag any night of the week, without him noticing. After an evening at Suze's house, the solitude at mine could be overwhelming.

When my folks died, Suze and her mom begged me to come and stay with them. I couldn't though. Not for more than a few days. While I enjoyed the high energy level next door, I craved the calm and order of my family home. But with my parents gone, it was just too much. When I sold it a few months later, I found an apartment in a quiet neighborhood and set about recreating a similar vibe, albeit on a much smaller scale. Neat and tidy, everything had a place, and I came to relish the solitude afforded by living alone.

Suze got married to a guy she met while still in college and a few years later, I met Robbie. The men in our lives never really hit it off. Suze's husband was a real guy's guy and loved to spend all of his spare time rotating between his mancave with the huge TV and extensive stereo setup, and his basement workshop with more power tools than Sears and Robbie was well, Robbie. Suze and I saw each other regularly and spoke on the phone at least daily. Putting all those miles between us would change things, for sure. But honestly? Once I made my decision, nothing could've stopped me. Not Robbie, not Susan, not even if the college changed its mind and offered me tenure. Once I made up my mind to go, I was already on my way.

But I still needed to get through the next several weeks. I was committed to my classes and would never have left my students mid semester, no matter what. Plus, I might need a good reference someday. I did cut back, however, on committee work and some of the meetings that had filled my weekly calendar for the last seven years.

"Screw them," I told Kate. "I'm here for the students, my students. I'll hold my classes and my office hours. That's all they'll get from me," I vowed. I was looking forward to getting away from this campus, to be honest. When you think about it, college campuses are pretty strange places. There are three distinct populations, all inherently at odds with each other. The students are the largest group, but they also hold the least amount of power. They show up, expecting to get educated and prepared for the real world. They understand in theory that they will need to work hard (no hassle, no tassel) but many are not prepared for the reality of campus life. They sleep through introductory classes held in 500-seat auditoriums. They fill blue books with answers to questions created by a book publisher. They pay hundreds of dollars for textbooks that they may never need to actually open, and pull all-nighters finishing papers that can sit ungraded on the back seat of their professor's car for weeks. They complain to the administrators about how unfairly a particular professor treats them but nothing changes. Their parents nag them about their grades and although they can't wait to finish, many worry about what will become of them in the real world.

The administrators and staff are next and they are a force to be reckoned with. This group includes the president, vice presidents, directors, and all their minions. They perform essential functions without which the institution would fall apart: Admissions, Financial Aid, Registrar, Human Resources, Campus Police, Residence Life, Maintenance, Food Service. The latter two groups wield much power. Want to cause a revolt on a college campus? Change the type of toilet paper used or the brand of coffee served. Or start construction projects at various locations around the campus and tie up both car and pedestrian traffic. Cut back on the number of staff parking spaces. Things will get ugly really fast.

Finally, there is the faculty. Academic freedom and tenure combine to make this elite group relatively bullet-proof. But it's lonely at the top. Students fear faculty members as they have the ultimate weapon as payback for all the incivility they witness in their classrooms—final grades! Staff employees often resent faculty for their cushy schedules and summers off. Administrators can't stand the fact that it is next to impossible to get rid of a tenured member of the faculty. Photos and barnyard animals are required. At least this is what I hear.

Buy hey, honestly? You shouldn't believe a word out of my mouth. Especially not right now. I had been dumped. I am a teacher scorned. So, I held my classes, met with students during my office hours, and graded their work. I maintained a low profile on campus, a far cry from the past few 'leading up to tenure' years. I attended roughly half of the meetings I was expected at and rarely spoke up. It was odd, watching people's reactions. Some of my students were visibly upset: the ones who had enjoyed my introductory classes were looking forward to my upper-level courses and having me supervise their internships, I wrote at least a dozen letters of reference for jobs and grad school the very first week after word got out that I was leaving. But my colleagues? Not very collegiate. Apparently, the news had leaked while I was still at the conference and most of the faculty and staff knew about my impending doom before I did. It's like I was contagious or something. Like *failure to get tenure* was catching. No one ignored me exactly, but few got close either, especially the three other faculty members who *were* granted tenure that spring. Apparently other teaching disciplines were ranked as more critical than marketing. Kate stayed awkward and apologetic, and the rift between Linda and me continued to grow. I was okay with all of this. I had gotten very used to being alone and I had a lot going on in my personal life. I was convinced that I was going to a better place. This crap was only temporary. I was busy and excited and had lots of 'to do' lists to complete every day. I do like my lists. Sometimes when I do something not on my list, I write it in and then cross it off. You too?

The days flew by and weekends were spent organizing and paring down. Except for Saturday mornings, of course. They were sacred, spent with Robbie. I started a countdown—only five more Saturdays, four, three. The rest of the time I was busy, but not crazed. I was determined to minimize and just relocate the essential items that I loved. As I had no real idea of what I would be doing or how I would spend my time after I arrived, I got rid of just about everything that I didn't know if I would need.

"It's like *déjà vu* all over again," I grumbled to a neighbor when she saw me heading for the dumpster in the back of our building for the third time that day. "I feel like I just did all this and here I am doing it again." Because I had. I had lived in my current place for only eighteen months. Why do we collect so much stuff? Who really needs three sets of everyday dishes and all these pans? I'm the guru of consumer behavior, at least on my campus, but even I was puzzled by all that I had accumulated over the years. I unearthed four pie plates. Four! And I don't even like pie. Except Boston cream, that is. Of course, that's really cake, yes?

But back to packing. *Less is more*, I told myself. I kept one of the pie plates, gave a painted ceramic one to Suze, and put the other two in the donate pile. *When I get to Sedona* became my new mantra. *When I get to Sedona*, I'll find a small, bright, and sunny space and fill it only with things I love. *When I get to Sedona*, I'll start exercising again and be more careful about what I eat. I had been indulging in fast food on a regular basis ever since I came back from the conference. Meal planning, shopping, and cooking just didn't seem to be priorities those last couple of months. I had plans to finalize, things to do, people to see, but I swore that once I got to Sedona, I would get back to being healthy again. Maybe a small garden, I fantasized. I could grow my own vegetables, go organic, maybe adopt that whole vegetarian thing. Like Rick. Or vegan. Robbie laughed at me when I shared my thoughts during one of our Saturday lunches.

"Man, I can't even imagine. You? Without a burger? That doesn't sound pretty." I put down my cheeseburger and answered him crossly.

"You don't know. When I get to Sedona, maybe I'll never have another cheeseburger again." I might have been more convincing but for the ketchup goatee I was sporting.

"But maybe you'll miss those cheeseburgers," he said. I picked up on what he was saying. I'm very adept at reading between the lines. See, we were no longer talking about meat on a roll.

"But what if those cheeseburgers are holding me back?" I asked, only half kidding. Robbie had no quick response for once, and I changed the subject to 'French fries and why it was better to share them.' Safe. But that afternoon after lunch, he came back to my apartment with me and we spent the next several hours in bed together. Sex was slower and more tender than usual. Robbie cupped my face in his hands.

"I'll miss you, Cheeseburger," he said. "More than you know." I kind of nodded and snuffled my assent. I knew that teasing or sarcasm, well; it just wasn't the right time.

"I know." I told him. "Ditto."

So, the weeks flew by and I continued to make my plans. I called to have my cable and landline service terminated. Both Susan and Robbie offered (separately) to make the drive with me and then fly home. But it would have to be an either-or. I knew that neither of them would consider being stuck together in a car for that long. I could just imagine the constant bickering, so I didn't even ask. I would have to choose just one of them. I swear *Sophie's Choice* couldn't have been more complex or fraught with emotional landmines. Although it sounded good and probably made some sense to have a co-pilot, I couldn't choose. And besides, I needed to do this alone. I needed to drive into town on my own and start my life over. I figured out where I would probably stop and spend the night during the four or five days that I estimated it would take me to get to Sedona. I even considered scheduling ahead and reserving a room in those destinations, but I didn't. *Be more spontaneous*, I told myself, let it go. Stop planning everything. Live in the moment. I decided to just wing it, but not without a GPS. I'm trying to be more flexible, I'm not bat-shit crazy.

The last couple of weeks at work seemed to drag, but they actually flew by. In the years I had spent at the college, I apparently made quite a number of friends, most of whom now wanted to take me out for lunch, meet me for drinks, or have me over for dinner. Now that I was just about gone, everyone liked me again. In the end, I wasn't the co-worker who didn't fit, the odd man out. I was that mystical, desirable colleague who was moving on. And sunny Arizona would be a nice place to visit during those cold New England winters. You never know, might as well end things on a positive note. But I was restless and ready to go.

So, I went.

CHAPTER 7

♫ The Way We Were ♫

'm not sure we ever *really* wanted kids ... I mean it's just not something we ever got around to doing. With my parents as role models, can you really blame me? Robbie wasn't super close with his folks either. They had split up when he was a teenager. Years of being put in the middle of the war that that raged between them, being forced to celebrate two of every holiday, and dealing with step-parents to boot, he was pretty much checked out on the whole family thing. In our seven years of marriage, the subject rarely came up. We were a career couple, you know? Actually, we had both claimed to want kids, but not that much, and never at the same time. We had married shortly before I turned thirty-one. Clock ticking, I half assumed that we would start a family right away. But then Robbie got promoted and was almost never home. I buckled down at work and found myself loving academic life. Sixteen credits shy of a bachelor's degree made Robbie a tad defensive about attending academic work functions with me, and with him so often out of town, I started going to most events on my own. There was always something ... a colleague was promoted or published and we needed to celebrate. A visiting author or guest speaker was in town. An opening in the department prompted a spate of dinner interviews. I never said "No." I always said "Where?" or "What time?" When Robbie did join me, it was awkward. He didn't fit in. I knew it and so did he. So did my colleagues. He came across as too glib, too smooth. He wasn't, but he seemed superficial around my earnest, rather shabby crew of co-workers. An hour into dinner at my department chair's home and my very extroverted, very lovely husband would be hissing at me.

"You said we'd just stay for drinks. You promised, Jackie." Torn between wanting to appease my husband and needing to make a favorable impression, I felt like I was being pulled apart. I would beg him to be patient.

"Just twenty minutes, okay? What's twenty minutes, huh?" Sometimes I would make our excuses to the host.

"He has an early flight, you know?" Once, I just ignored Rob, and he proceeded to get drunk. Not rip-roaring or scene-making drunk. Just quietly, morosely hammered. Enough to fall asleep on an overstuffed armchair in the den. When I found him there later that evening, I felt such a range of emotions. Exasperation that he was such a poor sport, relief that I had been able to stay for the entire party, and fear that we really were growing apart. *What did it mean that my husband and I had so little in common?* I stuffed him into the car and by the time we arrived home, he was sober enough to make it into the house and collapse on the sofa. I slept alone that night and we never spoke about it again. Not once. But we really started to go our separate ways after that. I stopped asking him to accompany me anywhere. I threw myself into work and told myself we were fine and sometimes I actually believed me.

Robbie was busy, too. When he was in town, he frequently had clients to entertain. Even without a degree, my charming husband had been working his way up the ladder at a prestigious local advertising agency. That meant dinners and drinks, or tickets to a game or a show. Late nights, rich food, and lots to drink. As his wife, it was expected that I would frequently be present. I tried to keep up, at first.

"Sure, I'll go. Sounds good," I would respond brightly to his midday phone calls. I would dash home, fix my hair, apply some makeup, and rummage through the back of my closet for something dressy so that I could accompany my handsome husband for a night on the town. At first, I'd skim the newspaper or try to catch the news, looking for some tidbits to liven up my conversations.

"Something other than academia," Robbie said, "It always comes out like a lecture." That stung. I rarely commented on my work after that. I'm sure some of the folks I met assumed I stayed home or did volunteer work. Like I was a lady who lunched. *As if.* But it was really hard for me. After a couple of hours of forced laughter and gaiety, I was spent. It wasn't like one of my academic functions. Here I was the odd man out. With my serviceable looks, sensible shoes, and rather serious demeanor, I was not the person that his clients expected. I mean, I'm attractive enough. And I'm outgoing and all. I was really good at remembering names and faces. Comes from having a new lineup of students every semester. I would start off the night really well, ignoring the looks of surprise when Robbie would introduce me to someone new, enthusiastically shaking hands with those I had met before. Quick embraces, air kisses. "You look wonderful. How was the trip? How are the kids?" I never asked about spouses who weren't present, never asked, "When are you due?" unless a pregnancy was confirmed to my face. In short, I was the perfect corporate wife. When pressed, I could turn out a respectable spread of appetizers and drinks, and had two caterers on speed dial. Well, not really. But I knew the names of two caterers and how to contact them. It just wasn't my thing. It was hard to contradict my minimalist sensibilities and I really didn't connect with most of the people I met. Too phony, too transparent, and shallow. Not Robbie, though, he was the real deal. We went on for years like this. I knew something was wrong, something was missing, just not what. Our lives were too frequently out of sync. It hadn't always been like that, you know. We were a good couple once, maybe even a great couple.

We met at a career fair that my college was holding for our soon-to-be graduates. I was representing the School of Business on a panel made up of three faculty members and three business professionals. Robbie was one of the professionals. We each had several minutes to introduce ourselves and talk about opportunities in our field. I had barely noticed Robbie as we were seated at opposite ends of the long table facing the auditorium. Even after he was introduced and began speaking, I found myself restless and unable to give the other speakers my full attention. What was I doing there? Well, I was low man on the totem pole in my department trying to make my way onto the tenure track, so that was why I was picked. I had lectures to prep and exams to grade. I really did *not* want to be there. Then I heard one of the panelists say how a four-year degree wasn't all it was cracked up to be, and how he never graduated from college and was making a six-figure salary and wasn't even thirty. I couldn't believe that anyone could be so reckless. I sputtered and before I could stop myself, blurted out something like:

"Now wait a minute. Surely, you're not suggesting that our students drop out of college, are you?" Only it sounded more like:

"Nowwaitaminutesurelyourenotsuggestingthatourstudentsdropoutofcollegeareyou?"

My fellow panelist was gracious and calm, which flustered me even more. He chuckled and held up a hand in protest.

"No, certainly not, Miss? Ms?"

"Professor," I retorted.

"No, Ms. Professor, I was only trying to say that while a degree is a good thing to obtain, real life experience counts, too."

"We encourage our students to complete internships or field studies," I countered.

"That's excellent," he replied smoothly. "Maybe my firm can sponsor a student or two."

Before I could respond, the moderator jumped in and asked if anyone had questions. Countless questions later, most of which were directed at the anti-education panelist, the moderator thanked us for our input and declared the session a success. I gathered my bag, a folder with notes that I never referred to, and my cardigan (auditoriums can be very chilly even in April) and made my way toward the exit.

"Excuse me, Miss Professor?" I turned to face the boyishly handsome man who had hijacked the recent session. *Wow, he was really good looking.* How had I missed that?

"What, hi. Can I help you?" He held out his hand in greeting.

"It's Robert, Robert Colby. Robbie to my friends."

"Hello, Robert," I replied. "I'm Jackie, Jax to my friends."

His face scrunched up in confusion.

"Jacks, like in the game?"

"Yeah, sure. Close enough." I replied. "Well, good to meet you." He followed me towards the exit.

"All that talking made me thirsty. Can I buy you a drink?"

"It's a dry campus, "I replied "and isn't it a little early to start drinking?" I could be such a tight-ass like that.

"Not if you've had the kind of week I have," he said. "How about an espresso or something like that?" *Caffeine!* Now you're talking.

"There are plenty of places for coffee on and off campus," I responded. "Why do you need me?"

"I didn't say I needed you, but I would like to make it up to you, and I hate to drink alone."

"Make *what* up to me?"

"C'mon. I have a feeling that didn't go as you planned."

"What tipped you off?" I asked sarcastically. "When you told our students to drop out of school or when you made a complete mockery of the rest of the panel?" Apparently, I was a drama queen as well as a tight-ass.

"Hold on now, Jackie. That's not what I said. You're assuming the worst about me." All the while we were arguing, we were walking towards the Visitors' parking lot. He stopped by a red, late-model sports car.

"This is me. Can I drop you?" I smirked at the image of this brash, flashy guy driving a car that was *soooo* him. Of course, this was his.

"Nice wheels," I huffed. I hoped my tone was dripping with sarcasm.

"Thanks," he replied. "Let's grab some lunch."

I honestly don't know what prompted me but some little voice said, 'Do it. Get in.' So, I did. He took me to a small seafood place I had never been to. Over bowls of chowder and really terrific crab cakes, we shared our stories. Found we actually had lots in common. Well music, really: early Dave Matthews, 60's rock and roll, and the sounds of Al Green. Counting Crowes over The Black Crows, more REM, less Nirvana. The Beatles *and* the Stones. It was not an either-or. Neither of us had any tolerance for reality TV. We both liked movies and many of the same ones. Both only children. His parents had each remarried and both lived in Florida with their new spouses. He seemed saddened by the fact that both my parents were deceased.

"You're all alone," he said in amazement.

"Well, not really, but yeah I guess so." He covered my hand with his. I was delighted to feel a slight tingle when he did. Also, that he didn't say something cheesy like, "Well you're not alone anymore." Cue the violins.

We were never really apart much after that. We walked around for a while, got that drink, talked some more, and ended up at my place. A few weeks later, he moved some of his things in and a few months later, gave notice on his apartment and moved in with me. We got married at the beginning of the year during semester break and managed a three-day honeymoon in Vermont. And that, as they say, was that.

Robbie was easy to be around, easy to talk to, run errands with, and chill out on Sunday mornings with. He was fine staying in on the nights he didn't have a work function. After fixing a simple stir fry together or grilling burgers or shrimp, I would retire to my office to grade papers or prepare for the next day's classes. He would stretch out on the recliner and watch TV. Sports sometimes or reruns of macho classics like *The A-Team* or *Miami Vice*. Around nine, he'd bring me in a mug of hot tea or an ice-cold glass of lemonade. I would take a break and before long, join him in the bedroom. Sex was easy, too. Robbie was always ready, always eager to please, and for the first time ever, I was relaxed and comfortable. He even convinced me that I was beautiful, desirable, hot. Okay, not hot, exactly. But he wanted me and he loved me. Probably still does. I knew it then and I know it now, I think.

Life was good. I was happy and I know he was, too. We made a good couple and had a nice life together for a while. At the end of the day—a day of students and lectures and grading and department meetings—he was the only person I wanted to see, to talk to. He got me, had my back, shared my foxhole, you know?

But all good things have to come to an end, right? Yeah, they do. It's the rules. I don't write them. I just have to follow them. We all do. I think in the end, we just couldn't escape from our pasts. I couldn't stop comparing our marriage, our relationship with that of my parents and we kept coming up short. Robbie seemed convinced that he was bound to follow his father's path of failed relationships, and probably just accepted that a divorce was inevitable. We never really fought with each other and never tried to fight for each other, either. We had our nice life together. Now we have to have our nice lives apart.

CHAPTER 8

♫ Time for Me to Fly ♫

I arrived without incident. I love the sound of that phrase. Simple and elegant, yes? Sad? Hell yeah. I wish that I could say that the drive was memorable, *with* incident—of the good kind, I mean. After all, it's the journey, not the destination, right? I wish I could say that the old guy at the general store who gave me directions was wise in the ways of the world. That he knew so much more than just how to get back to the interstate, that he gave me a glimpse into the real meaning of life. Or that the wise-cracking, big-hearted waitress at the coffee shop scooped me an extra helping of ice cream to à *la mode* my homemade bread pudding with a conspiratorial wink in her eye, like we shared the same dreams. Really, I wish I could say these things. But, I can't. That would be a lie and I rarely lie without a really good reason.

By the time I reached *my final destination* as the airlines say, I had driven 2,500 miles in my new car, bought just before I left. It lost that new car smell within the first few days, replaced by the lingering scent of road fumes, fast food wrappers and spilled coffee. In about 45 hours of driving over nearly five days, I had the bare minimum of personal contact, if you don't count the hand gestures from the long-distance truckers who I really pissed off by not going more than 70mph, even when I could. Since I rarely vacated the middle lane, the road was lonely. A different hotel desk clerk greeted me at the end of each long day of driving. One night I splurged. I found a five-star hotel outside of Tulsa. I was craving luxury and creature comforts. I unearthed a bathing suit scrunched up in the bottom of the fourth suitcase I dug through then sat in a steamy hot tub nursing a glass of white wine for nearly an hour. *Don't try this at home, boys and girls.* Alcohol and hot tubs are *not* meant to go together. But they do, they really do. I ordered pasta and a Caesar salad from room service and enjoyed both at my little table on my little balcony overlooking a golf course, swathed in a plush terry cloth robe. I was in the robe, not the golf course. Talk about the dangers of misplaced modifiers. The meal seemed even more scrumptious due to the fact that it was the first one I had not unwrapped or eaten with a plastic spork (don't even get me started) in three days. Actually longer, because the last couple of days at home had been spent packing and eating leftover pizza and a couple of fast-food breakfast sandwiches. Don't judge me, all my pans were packed or donated by then. Robbie and Suze had been acting kind of territorial and weird about my "last night" in town. Not wanting to choose, I bailed on both of them.

I actually avoided Robbie that last week. He seemed sad and more serious than I was used to and it was getting really awkward hiding how excited I was. *Or about whom.* I was never good at keeping secrets, actually, especially from Robbie. I can keep a confidence for someone else. You can always trust me to keep mum. But when I had something personal to share, good or bad, it was almost impossible to keep it in. I knew that if he tipped my chin and looked into my eyes, I would blurt out that I was hot for a tour guide I had known for a total of three hours almost ten weeks ago. So, I kept the talking to a minimum, preferring to demonstrate between the sheets just how much I would miss him. Action speaks louder than words. I am full of homilies and platitudes today. And I would, miss him I mean. And Suze? I was exhausted from all of the emotion I was fielding on her behalf. My normally calm, serene bestie of more than twenty-five years was losing it. The closer I got to leaving, the calmer I got. Not Suze. She would call me crying.

"What am I going to do without you? I can't even imagine it." The different time zones really got to her. What's two hours between friends? I swore that she could wake me with an early morning phone call any time she wanted. Texting, Skyping, emails. We would meet up, visit, talk on the phone.

"But it won't be the same, Jax," she always countered. I almost reconsidered her offer to drive out with me and then fly home, but I didn't. I needed to do this on my own.

By do this, I mean drive in a semi-hypnotic state through Erie, Columbus, St. Louis, Oklahoma City, and the aforementioned Tulsa. I checked in daily with Suze, but kept our conversations brief. I left messages for Robbie on his landline during the day when I knew he wouldn't be home and then ignored his return calls. *Passive-aggressive much?* I would later blame fatigue, white line fever, heavy traffic. But the truth of the matter? I was scared shitless. I was way beyond having second thoughts. Tenth thoughts, infinity thoughts. *What was I doing and why?* I would try to fix on Rick's face and sometimes I couldn't really remember what he even looked like. Would he remember me? Hell. Would I even recognize him? I almost called him. Several times. I had memorized what I believed to be his cell phone number, but each time I froze. It was panicky fear. Pure and simple. I was nervous and edgy and the calm that had permeated my mind and the sureness with which I had conducted the last few weeks were gone, replaced with panic.

It began when I woke each morning. I was instantly awake, dry-mouthed and heart hammering, sweat-soaked sheets and everything. I would map out the day's route after showering and getting my morning caffeine fix. My fear would subside to a more manageable low level of dread. If I hadn't been trying to concentrate on the road, I would have been glancing over my shoulder. Nervous and twitchy, I switched radio stations constantly and bemoaned the fact that I hadn't taken Robbie up on his offer to order a satellite radio subscription for me before I left. I hate to say it, but there is a whole lot of nothing between here and there.

By the end of a long day on the road, punctuated by stops for more coffee, fast food, and bathroom breaks, my panic would start to resurface. By the time I pulled into the Holiday Inn Express *du jour*, my palms would be sweaty and my heart would be pounding. Exhausted, I would shower, pick at the take-out meal I had purchased right before I checked in and zone out in front of the TV. Too restless to sit still and too exhausted to go for a walk or check out the advertised exercise room, I was glad for only one thing. I was alone. I didn't have to convince anyone that I was doing the right thing or cover up how anxious and tense I was feeling. No need to fake it or keep up appearances. I was glad that the two people who knew me the best and loved me the most in spite of what they knew, were not there to witness what I was going through. It sucked.

"Taking lots of pictures?" Suze inquired brightly one morning. *Yeah right.* I snapped a couple later that day with my phone but they weren't of anything memorable. I was going through the motions. It was all about the destination for me. Screw the journey.

I started to perk up around the time I reached Albuquerque. The scenery, which had been fairly forgettable until that point, started to interest me. Started looking like I was smack in the middle of the Southwest. And I was. I took a selfie in front of a cactus on the side of the road about twenty miles from Flagstaff and sent it to Robbie and Suze's phones. Robbie called me within minutes.

"Almost there," I trilled.

"I'm proud of you, Jaxie," Robbie told me. "You saw what you wanted and you made it happen." *Whom* I wanted, I amended silently and told him I would touch base later. I felt a twinge of remorse as I hung up the phone. Robbie. I wasn't 100% certain, but I didn't think that he had dated very much since our split. Not because he wasn't a catch. He was, is. Boyish good looks, trim athletic build, funny, sweet. If he did date, he was discreet. Not that he needed to be. We were divorced. Split. Living separate lives. But not really.

As I got back in the car for the last fifty or so miles of my trip, my thoughts weren't on Rick, whatever he looked like. I was thinking of Robbie, my ex-husband and best friend. I hoped he would meet someone special and relatively soon. Someone young enough to maybe start a family with or maybe a widow with teenagers. A ready-made family. How convenient. Robbie could play video games with the kids and teach them how to … well, honestly, Robbie didn't have the type of skills that a single mom might be looking for in a father figure for her kids. Sexist of me? Yeah, maybe. But come on. He is useless at fixing things and has, at best, a rudimentary knowledge of automobiles and power tools. He could spend $100 at the grocery store within minutes of stopping to pick up a loaf of bread. Honestly. But he was and is a good, good man with a great big heart and an ability to make whomever he was talking to feel lucky. Lucky that they got to spend time with him. He excelled at his job, balancing creative duties along with those required to maintain and grow accounts. He could paint a ceiling, balance a checkbook, and throw together a veritable feast out of odds and ends in the fridge. And in bed? I shivered. That widow would be counting her lucky stars. She would be small, curvy, dark-haired. That was his type, actually. Not long, lanky, almost a ginger, like me. I pictured Mrs. Colby 2.0 in my mind. *Shit. No, not happening.* She would be graying a little, maybe a bit thicker around the middle after all those kids, not shopping in the junior department for years now. A sensible woman, kind and sweet. Grateful. And maybe he wouldn't have to meet her quite yet. What's the rush?

I had plenty of evidence to support my hypothesis that my ex crushed on Natalie Wood lookalikes. Evidence I had viewed years ago in the form of his mom's photographs: a seemingly endless array of petite, stacked brunettes possessively clutching his arm or gazing adoringly into his hazel eyes. Photo after photo, starting from an eighth-grade dance (God, his thirteen-year-old date was built. I am a grown-ass woman and I'll never have boobs like that) all the way through adulthood. Rarely the same girl twice, I realized. Every 'first' in his young life was captured in all of its celluloid splendor. First dance, first car, high school graduation, first apartment. Every photo depicting my handsome soul mate looking happy, relaxed, and oh so young. Where had all of these non-blondes come from? Where had they gone? Why were acid-washed jeans ever popular? I had always assumed that young Robbie had been very popular, one of the cool kids. And here was proof. Even after all these months together, I was still thrilled and more than a little surprised that he wanted me to sit with him at the cool kids' table, as it were. It had been an awkward enough afternoon even without the damn photos. I had spent most of it on the couch with Robbie's mother, being grilled and apparently found wanting in every aspect of my sorry existence. All the fun took place at her home in Florida before we were married—the first time I met her. Robbie and I had planned a long weekend trip for me to meet his family.

Following a couple of days at the sprawling Disney complex in Orlando, we drove to his mom's house for lunch. Jean and her second husband, Don lived in a roomy condo in a senior retirement community. Over shrimp salad and sweet tea, we exchanged pleasantries and made small talk. Robbie resembled his mom in coloring but he must have gotten his height from his dad, as she was itty-bitty. Feeling like a large and gangly moose, I followed her into their sun room (I guess you only call them Florida rooms when you're not actually in Florida) when Robbie agreed to a tour of the facilities with Don in their new golf cart.

"Our time for girl talk," Jean promised. She wasted no time on small-girl talk. It was big-girl talk, all the way. The door closed on the two men and she pounced. Within minutes, I was praying for Robbie's return. I saw his cell where he had left it on the breakfast bar, so I couldn't even call him. 'Come get me,' I prayed. Her rapid-fire questioning revealed the following: I was thirty-years old, never married, no children (that I knew about—she didn't even crack a smile and this was some of my best material), had a year-to-year contract at a so-so college teaching people how other people shopped (huh?), both parents deceased, no political party affiliation, and lacking any organized religious background. Yeah, that's me. *What a catch!*

Satisfied that she knew enough, she pulled out the big guns, her prized photo albums. No shots of a baby on a bearskin rug or her little guy learning to ride a two-wheeler. No, these albums featured my boyfriend with all of his old girlfriends. Apparently, each had made a favorable impression on his mom. *She* was a lovely girl. Oh, *she* was the head cheerleader. *She* loved to bake for Robbie. Each girl she pointed out had been outstanding in one way or another. And finally, the *pièce de résistance*. A glossy 8 x 10 featuring the prom king and queen.

"Robbie and Libby," Jean breathed reverently. "They were such a beautiful couple. She was like a little doll, beautiful. Lovely in every way and sooo sweet."

"Hmmm," I agreed. She *was* lovely and a dead ringer for; you guessed it—Natalie Wood. Sensing my lack of sincerity, Jean regarded me severely.

"Everyone assumed they would get married. They were a match made in heaven." Alrighty then.

"Whatever happened to Libby?" I asked innocently.

"She broke my boy's heart," she responded sadly. "She left for college and got pregnant in her first semester. She had to drop out. She married the guy and moved with him to Ohio." Out of thin air, a hankie had appeared which she used to dab at her misty eyes.

"Ohio's not *that* bad," I wanted to say. But I was nice.

"Well, that was a long time ago," I consoled her. "Robbie's moved on. Moved in ... with me. You do know we're engaged, right?" She sniffed, unconvinced. Geez, I wanted to like her. To love her. She had raised Robbie with precious little help from his dad, who bailed when Robbie was only ten. He reappeared at Robbie's twelfth birthday party, uninvited and with a red-headed stripper, or at least a red head who dressed like a stripper. But I digress. Emotionally spent and unwilling to moon over any more photos of my beloved, I finally saw a chance to escape. Overwhelmed by the memory of the one who got away, Jean leaned back on the overstuffed sofa. I used the opportunity to make a sweeping grab for the offending photo album. I slammed it shut, hopped up, and leapt across the room. Like a graceful gazelle, really.

"Think I'll go check on the guys," I told her and darted out the door. An hour later, I thanked her for lunch and a "lovely" visit. The transformation had begun. *Lovely* had apparently become my go-to adjective of choice. I bent over and kissed her smooth, unlined cheek. I didn't want her to think poorly of me. I wanted her to like me and to know that I would take good care of her son.

"I love him," I whispered in her ear.

"I'm sure you do," she responded, patting my hand somewhat sympathetically. *Game on bitch!*

I faked a nap on the drive to the hotel to avoid a conversation. How do you tell your fiancé that you hate his mother and that the feeling is apparently quite mutual? Answer? You don't. I hoped that dinner with Robbie's dad that evening would go better. I needed to connect with at least *one* of his parents, didn't I?

"Don't get your hopes up, Jax," Robbie warned me as we drove to the restaurant that evening. "Honestly, he can't be trusted. I wouldn't be surprised if he stood us up." But he didn't. Robert, Senior was tall, tan and fit. Sporting a pink polo shirt, white pants, and shoes with no socks, he looked like he would be more at home in a country club than the noisy, happening little bistro he had picked out.

"Jackie, so nice to finally meet you. I've heard good things." Really? From whom? Father and son barely spoke, save for a terse phone call arranging tonight's logistics. He went in for a hug, but I thrust my arm out, awkwardly blocking him. His grip was pulverizing.

"Rob, looking good," he boomed. Robbie's reply was curt and just this side of rude. We settled at a table that would have been tight for two people and ordered a round of drinks. The restaurant was loud, packed with noisy people, and even though we were nearly on top of each other, it was hard to hear. Conversation at a minimum, I had ample opportunity to study the man who made my fiancé so crazy. The one person in the world he had so little patience for. I gotta hand it to Senior. He attempted to keep up a dialogue, despite the din of the restaurant, but Robbie wasn't having it. I sat between the two of them and witnessed the same dynamic that had probably characterized their relationship for years. Father and son. The cat's in the cradle. Too little, too late.

Robbie's mood alternated between guarded, pissed off, and totally bored. I kicked him under the table once when he yawned without apologizing, but I'm not at all certain that I actually made contact. And then things got really interesting. Shelley, Senior's latest squeeze, just *happened* to stop by and agreed to join us for dessert. How lovely. At that point, Robbie totally shut down and tuned us out, ordering a brandy, which I had never seen him do before. Shelley finally got up to use the "little girl's room." Yeah, she really said it. She seemed surprised and a bit sad when I turned down her request to come with her.

"I don't have to go," I told her honestly. Watching her sashay across the crowded restaurant, Senior looked to his son for confirmation.

"What do you think?" he asked hopefully. "Isn't she something?" Robbie sneered openly at his father and wondered aloud whether Senior should adopt her or send her off to a good boarding school. In Senior's defense, she wasn't *that* young. Younger than Robbie and me, sure, but hardly jailbait. In Robbie's defense, his dad had apparently been parading a series of increasingly younger twinkies for his son's approval since that horrible birthday party. At some point, Senior had actually married one of them, Edie, who was expecting us for brunch in the morning. *Will this fun never end?* Robbie apparently adored his stepmother Edie and knowing that his dad had unceremoniously dumped her last year fueled his anger even more.

"He's useless," he had fumed at the time. "He just left her, just like my mom."

We made our excuses shortly thereafter. Well, I did anyway, and expressed gratitude for the lovely meal that Senior insisted on paying for. While I air-kissed and pseudo-hugged the beaming couple, Robbie stood off to the side and waited for the valet to bring our rental car around. I half expected him to peel out away from the curb as a juvenile but effective way of demonstrating just how pissed off he was, but he didn't.

As we drove back to the hotel, I was grateful for the cool darkness of the car. I was glad to be out of that bustling over-priced, over-chic supper club with its artificial brightness and annoying clamor. I avoided conflict like the plague and hated witnessing anyone I loved embroiled in it. Robbie did not seem to be free of it, however. He hadn't yet shaken off the family drama of the evening. He stared straight ahead and handled the steering wheel with a death grip. His clenched jaw and rigid posture left no doubt that it had been a rough evening. He shrugged off my attempts at conversation and upon returning to our room, paced its length as I busied myself in the bathroom, removing my makeup and brushing my teeth. I slipped into a lightweight nightie and then offered to slip out of it, trying to seduce my very tense sweetheart. *Epic fail!* Rejecting my advances, he mumbled something about needing air. Clueless as I could be at times, even I knew better than to offer to accompany him. I lay in bed for what seemed like hours wondering where he was and what he was doing. I wasn't worried *per se,* but I felt badly that his relationship with his dad was even more broken than I had believed.

I must have fallen asleep at some point as I was suddenly aware that Robbie was beside me, sound asleep on his back. Reeking of beer (and was that cigarette smoke?) my beloved slept fitfully and snored lightly. Grateful for his return and wanting him to feel safe and loved, I snuggled up next to him and fell into a deep sleep.

The next morning, we showered and had coffee and bagels from room service. Conversation was kept to a minimum. Later, driving to Edie's suburban home, he reached over and grasped my hand.

"Sorry, Jax," he said. "I just …"

"I know, Rob, I know. It's okay." I reassured him. He seemed much better this morning. More relaxed, more, well, Robbie. We only had to drive for a half hour or so to get to Edie's. She lived in an airy townhome in an exclusive neighborhood. Not a retirement community, I judged, based on the basketball hoops, bicycles, and strollers that populated the neighbors' lots. Not a senior citizen, I realized when Edie opened the door and allowed her stepson to sweep her up in a big hug. Early to mid-forties maybe. Wow—she was stunning. So, when Rob was 16, she was maybe 30? *Hmmm*.

Later, after a delicious meal featuring all of Robbie's favorites (I had apparently underestimated my future mate's penchant for French toast and turkey sausage) I leaned back contentedly in my chair.

"If I was wearing a belt, I'd have to loosen it," I told Edie. "All we've done since we've been here is eat."

"How was last night?" Edie casually asked. Robbie laughed.

"The grouper was fresh, the conversation? Not so much."

"Oh Rob." Edie took his hand, "He's not that bad."

"I love it, you're defending him. After all he's done."

"He did those things to me, Rob, and to your mom. You were um, collateral damage, I guess."

"The guy's a jerk and I'm an idiot for even thinking he'll change, be a standup guy, actually stick around."

Edie looked concerned but stopped defending her estranged spouse. Pissed off, but determined not to be, Robbie launched into a series of stories featuring his teen-aged self and the young pretty stepmother that he so obviously adored. One tale involved her making an early morning trip to the convenience store. Waking up early one morning and realizing that her seventeen-year-old stepson and a few of his friends had consumed several pitchers of screwdrivers the night before, Edie rushed off to purchase more orange juice so as not to anger her husband. She knew he'd be upset, not at the underage drinking, but at the lack of juice for his breakfast!

Over scores of grilled cheese sandwiches, Robbie had

bonded with his stepmom during a time when the war that had waged for years between his mother and father hit its peak. They fought over custody, finances, needed repairs on the house that Robbie and his mother still lived in, you name it. Nothing was off-limits. Robbie was frequently forced into the middle. Movie nights with Edie, doing homework under her supervision, mundane tasks like back-to-school shopping—Robbie cherished the time he spent with her. He even lived with them during college breaks once his mom remarried, sold the house, and moved to Florida. Edie had urged her husband to hold off on a similar move until Robbie was through college. But Rob dropped out in his senior year, got a full-time job in advertising, and moved in with a couple of friends. Shortly thereafter, Edie and Senior moved south, living just a half hour from Jean and her new husband. And here we were.

I got a big hug from my tiny, dark-haired soon to be ex, future, step mother-in-law.

"I've never seen him so happy, Jax." She told me. *Happy?*

"Not today so much, but whenever I talk to him on the phone. He's over the moon. I'm so glad for both of you."

I smiled at her and knew that she was responsible at least in part for raising the wonderful man I was going to marry.

"Thank you for everything," I told her. "I love him."

"And he loves you," she responded. "I know he does." *Good answer.* That's the reaction I had been hoping for. Rushing to get to the airport for our late afternoon flight home, I looked over at the love of my life.

"Anything you want to share about your relationship with Edie?" I teased. Robbie laughed out loud.

"Hey, back then, I would have let something happen, you know. And not just to get back at my dad, either. But I couldn't risk it. She was my best friend. Besides, she never thought about me like that anyway." *Yeah, right.* But I felt relieved. At least he was honest about his feelings, clichéd and twisted as they were.

But maybe a woman like Edie was in Robbie's future. He deserved a wonderful life. As I reached the Sedona city limits, I was ready to let go. It was time to move on.

'Be happy, Rob.' I silently messaged him across the miles. 'I am.' And I was.

CHAPTER 9

♫ Hello It's Me ♫

'll never be accused of being short, not just because I'm tall, but also because I tend to be wordy. My theory is simple. Why risk being misunderstood with a brief response when you can make your point over and over with a longer one? Honestly, there are precious few questions that can be adequately answered with a one or two word answer. Do you take this man or woman as your lawfully wedded husband or wife? Do you have something? Do you swear to tell the whole truth, the whole truth? You get the idea. I've never been confident enough, I guess, to be so clear or so certain that a short response would suffice, plus I wouldn't want to come across as terse or abrupt. Or curt. I like to cover all the bases. Have I made my point? It's no different in the classroom. I know my subject well and I relate to my students. I can tell stories and give lots of examples in order that everyone understands the more complex topics, but I can get to the point when I need to.

That's why it comes as such a surprise that with Rick, I feel so calm, so confident. I should be nervous, but I'm not. Maybe it's exhaustion from nearly five days on the road, but I was feeling very relaxed. I didn't feel the need to embellish or clarify anything. I had arrived at the Jeep tour office late in the afternoon shortly after getting to Sedona. I had debated calling him first, but since I'd held off all this time, I decided to just show up. I asked the receptionist if Rick Bowers was available and she assured me that his tour was due in shortly. I sat in the waiting room and thumbed through one of their brochures, when suddenly he was there. The receptionist must have pointed me out, because he crossed the lobby and walked right towards me. I jumped up and greeted him warmly. I told him I was glad to see him again. Initial surprise led to utter confusion on his part once it was obvious that I was not there to book a tour. When he asked me,

"What are you doing here?"

I said, "I moved here."

When he said "When?"

I said "Today."

When he asked "Why?"

I said "Why not?"

Scintillating conversation, I know, right? In response to his follow-up questions, I was still on a roll.

"I don't know. I'm not sure," and finally "Yes, I'm starving."

We left my car in the lot and walked down the street to a small Mexican restaurant. Rick seemed kind of nervous. Actually, like he'd seen a ghost. Like he should probably know me, but from where? He held it together while we were seated and handed menus. When Carla, our perky waitress brought him a Dos Equis in a frosty mug, however, he downed half of it like he was parched, then leaned forward and everything came tumbling out.

"But, seriously, what do you plan to do? How will you get by?" He seemed really anxious to hear my response. A sly smile came over me. I sat back in the vinyl booth and shrugged my shoulders.

"I figured I'd move in with you," I purred, channeling my former colleague, Linda.

"Oh wait, ha ha. Okay, I get it." Rick regained his composure and laughed nervously. I joined in and we shared a quick laugh, then got down to brass tacks. We ordered. Veggie burger for Rick, chicken quesadilla for me. We made small talk about the weather and I gave him a quick rundown on the route that I had taken.

"Yeah, that was good. That's the way I would have gone," he assured me. He seemed surprised at my extravagance when I told him about my night of luxury in Tulsa, but once our food got there, we busied ourselves eating. I was starved and the quesadilla was so good. Plus, I was starting to feel anxious and it gave me something to do.

"Guess I had to move here for good Mexican food, huh?" I offered. Rick had a mouthful, but seemed to nod in agreement. Intent on his burger, he was unaware that he had my full attention. I was able to truly study him for the first time. Green eyes? Check. Blond streaked hair? Check. Large brown hands and massive forearms. Oh yeah. Check. Check. He was even better looking than I remembered. Then Carla came over to offer refills.

"What's the good news?" she asked conversationally, as she brought a fresh round of drinks to our booth.

"It's our first date," I burst out. I was exhausted and punchy and seriously regretting my decision to not shower or at least freshen up before surprising Rick at work. It was the first thing I could think of. Carla squealed her approval.

"You two are such a cute couple," she beamed. Missing Rick's look of surprise, she zoned in and read the name which was embroidered over the pocket on his shirt and sang out,

"Rick and and ..." She was waiting for Rick to supply my name, but Rick was at a loss for words. I realized he was racking his brain for my name.

"Jackie," I told a now-confused Carla. "Rick and Jackie," I assured her. She beat a hasty retreat after that and I put my hand over Rick's.

"I was kidding. I don't know why I said that. It just slipped out. I'm kinda punchy, I guess." I tried to reassure him and calm the nervous drumming of his fingers. "Really, I was just kidding. Not about moving here, that's true, but I've always wanted to travel and after my trip out here this spring, it seemed like a great opportunity. When I popped in at the tour office just now, I just wanted to say hi. No pressure. I plan to relax and drink margaritas and enjoy myself for a while. I really need a break."

"But what about your job?" Rick asked. "You were a, a..."

"College professor," I supplied. *God, did he really not remember me at all?* "I don't have a job. I got turned down for tenure. That's kind of a big deal, you know. Getting tenure? Not always so much of a big deal, but NOT getting tenure, big deal."

"Why," Rick asked. "Why didn't you get it?" A crack about an inappropriate relationship with a student bubbled up but I restrained myself. I no longer felt calm or serene or even slightly in control. He didn't remember me. *Crap.*

"I don't know," I admitted. "Budget cuts, not doing enough publishing ... whatever. It was time for me to leave." He was looking at me with a really confused look on his face. *Uh-oh.* This was not good.

"Did you cut your hair?" he finally asked.

"Actually, I'm trying to grow it out."

"Well, you look different, somehow. Good, just different."
Uh-huh. He really didn't remember me. "Well, you look even better than all of my fantasies over the last ten weeks combined" was probably inappropriate and a bit over the top, I decided to change the subject to something less threatening.

"I need to check out some more affordable living arrangements. I can stay in the hotel for a while, but then I've got to figure something else out." Rick nodded sagely.

"Yeah, hotel bills can really add up. Which hotel?" I told him. He frowned.

"That's pretty expensive. I can name a few places easier on your budget."

"Oh, I know. But I got a really good severance so ..." Okay, that's a lie, colleges don't offer severance packages when you fail to make the grade, but Rick apparently didn't know that.

"Well, okay. I can try to get a better rate for you at least. We do it all the time. I'll make a call," he promised.

"Thanks so much. That would be awesome," I responded enthusiastically. "Then after that, any ideas for the long-term?"

"We're like family here," Rick assured me. "Everyone knows everyone in Sedona. Do you want an apartment? They're not that easy to find in town but Oak Creek or Cottonwood maybe. Sedona's tough." No, they sounded far away and not at all what I was looking for. I had moved *to* Sedona not *near* Sedona.

"Maybe room and board in a private house or something?" I wondered aloud. To say I had not given the matter of housing a single thought would not be an exaggeration. I was homeless and Rick was the only person I knew for more than a thousand miles.

"I'll check around," Rick offered. "I'll give you a call."

Satisfied that I was set for now and not looking to move in with him, Rick seemed to relax. We chatted amiably about the town and what drew us both in. He punched my number into his phone and seemed a bit surprised when I told him I already had his number. Rick finished his second beer and I was up to my eyeballs floating in Diet Coke. I really needed to use the ladies' room but a small part of me wondered if he would bolt the minute I did. *Real secure, huh?*

Rick started to tell me about the group he had just escorted. Two couples in their 60's from the Midwest on vacation. One of the women had just kept nagging at her husband.

"She never stopped once and he seemed so resigned, he just took it. The other couple didn't really seem like they liked each other very much either. I just don't get it."

"Marriage is tough," I said with a shrug.

"Yeah, just ask my ex-wife." My ears perked up at the mention of an ex.

"So, what about you?" Rick teased. "Any ex-husbands back home?"

"Just one." Robbie's face flashed before my eyes.

"Wait, are you blushing?" Rick asked. I *was* blushing. I could feel it. My cheeks felt hot and I was super conscious of Rick's eyes on me. I started to stutter.

"Well yes, I mean, you know … it, it's complicated. I don't know. I don't want to talk about it," I ended.

"Okay, no worries," Rick filled in smoothly. "I doubt my ex-wife ever wants to talk about me, either." *Whew, moving on.* With the skill and agility honed by many years toiling in the classroom as well as at cocktail parties, I brought the conversation back to a more neutral topic: me and what I was going to do next. Rick promised again to contact the hotel to get me a better rate. As I was already getting the AAA discount, I doubted he could, but I was pleased that he was willing to try for me. When Carla dropped off the bill and beat a hasty retreat without saying a word, I tried to pay.

"No way," said Rick, "Those effing tourists tipped really well and bedsides, I can't make you pay for your first dinner in Sedona."

"Okay, next one's on me," I promised, then immediately felt awkward as if I had suggested a second date. Or would that actually be our first date? Did our afternoon in the desert count? Rick didn't seem to notice my discomfort and we walked back to my car. He finally seemed comfortable. It was still my turn to be anxious. Really anxious. What's next? I wondered. Will he call? If so, when? I'm a thirteen-year-old girl waiting by the phone, I realized miserably.

"Okay then, uh … Jackie." I needed a name tag, I decided. A great big 'Hello, My Name Is' one.

"It's great to see you. I hope you enjoy Sedona." *Was he leaving? Was that it?*

"Oh yeah, okay," I said. "So, I guess I'll be seeing you." 'Don't cry,' I pleaded with myself. Not here. Walking away, Rick turned and waved.

"I'll call you," he said. "Have a good night and get some sleep. You look exhausted." I waved weakly, suddenly drained and totally spent. I slumped against my car.

"You gonna be okay?" he called. For a split second, he sounded just like Robbie.

"Sure," I assured him. "I'm just tired. It's been a long few days." Well, actually it's been a long few months, but that's okay. I'm here now. *Crap. I'm here now.* Rock? Meet hard place.

"I'll give you a couple days to get settled," Rick said. "Get some rest and we can touch base over the weekend. Okay?"

"Sounds good," I said, trying to sound breezy and casual and not intense and obsessive and stalkerish. "Okay, I'll talk to you then. Hey, thanks for dinner."

Rick smiled a great big tour guide smile. "Welcome to Sedona," he called out.

"See you, Rick." I had to shout, as he was a good distance away from me by then. I watched him sprint though the lot and let himself into the back door of the rental office with a key. I guessed that the office had closed while we were eating. But he has a key. Maybe he's like an assistant manager or something. What difference did it make? He didn't even remember me.

I drove slowly to the hotel. By the time I checked in, Rick had already worked his magic. The rate that I initialed was about $50 less per night than I had originally been quoted. He got me a deal, I thought. *Sweet.* I had moved 2,500 miles and he had made a phone call. Guess we're even. *Not!* I told the desk clerk I didn't need any assistance and made my way to the elevator carrying just my handbag and an overnight bag. The room was plush and dark and cool. *Perfect.* All the comforts of home: room service, a comfortable-looking bed, a good light to read by, and a huge flat screen TV. Oh, and an honor bar. As I tore into a Toblerone bar as long as my forearm, I remembered my vow. So much for 'Sedona me' with the healthy eating. I reasoned that this was only for a few days. I'd get settled and find a Whole Foods or someplace to stock up. But for now, a shower and maybe a cup of tea to wash down the candy. Chocolate throat, right?

After I showered and brewed a mug of tea with the little in-room unit, I flipped on the TV and curled up in clean sweats and a t-shirt. It didn't look like I had anything going on over the next couple of days, so I could get by with what

I had in my carry-on and leave my packed suitcases in the car. Tomorrow after breakfast, I vowed to take a drive and check out the area to make sure it was everything I hoped it would be. Maybe even get a head start on finding a place to live. Or I could wait a few days and see if Rick came through with any ideas. Sipping my tea, I got comfortable on the recliner in the corner and settled in to watch the local evening news. About halfway through the newscast, it hit me. I'm local. This is *my* local newscast. *Yikes.* Soon after, I dimmed the lights and slipped between crisp sheets. I slept well, for the first time I could recall.

After only six hours of sleep, I woke up fairly rested at five am. I chalked it up to the time difference and resisted the urge to crawl back under the covers. I dug in my bag for a pair of running shoes, brushed my teeth, and splashed cold water on my face. Time to check out the new neighborhood. I ran down four flights of stairs, zipped through the lobby, and once outside, breathed in cool fresh air. And I saw just how beautiful a Sedona sunrise could be. Like the news, *this* was local now. I would get to see this every day. Or at least on the days that I'm up this early … or out this late. I smiled. I could get used to this. And I started to.

CHAPTER 10

♫ Gimme Shelter ♫

Rick had been in heavy rotation at work for the past several days, which meant he was running four tours a day, starting at sunrise and ending with a sunset tour. On a normal day he would do two or three tours, but this was a particularly busy summer and lots of other guides had scheduled time off. The reason I mention this is because since our spur of the moment dinner my first night in Sedona, I had seen him only a couple of times for a quick coffee. Well, coffee for me, iced tea or lemonade for him. Oh, and he also helped me to move in to my new place which was really sweet of him.

On my third day staying at the hotel, he called me out of the blue. Told me that a friend of his had a guest house on his property and had agreed to rent it to the 'right person.' Rick assured him that it was me. I offered to drive out to the western edge of town and meet up with Edward 'Coop' Cooper that afternoon. Before I had even pulled into the driveway, I knew that this was the place for me. The lot was huge and the big house (although I'm sure the owner just called it the house) was gorgeous. Classic Sedona stucco with cacti dotting the professionally hardscaped lot. It was a great neighborhood and only a few blocks from a commercial district that looked hip and trendy. The guest house was on the back side of a large brick patio shared with the main house. No pool, but it looked fairly private with a separate carport of its own. It was much nicer than the places that I had found on Craigslist. I had driven by several rental properties over the last few days, but decided to see if Rick would come through before setting up any appointments. And he had. I hopped out of my car and looked around, not sure if I should approach the main house. I didn't have to wait long.

Seconds later, a slight grey-haired man came out of the guest house and waved to me. I crossed across the patio and shook hands with Edward Cooper. I followed him into the place that I hoped would become my new home. It was beautifully done, open-concept with high ceilings, glossy hardwood floors, and large windows. The main space featured a long marble breakfast bar that divided a cozy living area and a dining nook. The galley kitchen was well appointed with all of the high-end appliances of a much larger space. At the far end, a short hallway led to a lovely bathroom (with a tub) and a spacious bedroom with a large walk-in closet. I was thrilled with how nice it was and decided I would pay whatever exorbitant rent Edward was charging in order to live here. I knew that my furniture, currently in storage, would fit very nicely and imagined myself soaking in the Jacuzzi tub after a long day of hiking and four-wheeling and whatever other shenanigans I would be taking part in. I would need to purchase some barstools and a large area rug. *Oooh, time to shop!*

"Oh, it's perfect," I gushed. "Just lovely." This is me playing hard to get. It's quite an effective negotiating trick as long as you didn't mind paying more than the asking price. "And the views. I really love it."

Edward told me that he previously rented it out, then had overseen the renovations to the cottage in the hopes of enticing his daughter to visit. Apparently, that hadn't been successful, as he was now planning to rent it again. I hoped it would be to me. He said that we could go month-to-month and that a security deposit would be fine, but if I didn't have it, that would be okay, too.

"I'm right across the patio if you need anything and of course you've got Rick," he added. Did I *have* Rick?

"Oh no, it's not like that," I stammered. "We're just well, it's complicated." Edward looked suspicious.

"Rick vouched for you. He told me about your situation and said you were out of a job, but he said you'd be able to pay on time. Tell me now if that's not the case. After the last time, I swore I'd never rent this place again."

"Oh, no," I protested. "I can pay, that's not what I meant. Rick must've assumed that since I was divorced and had lost my job that I must be strapped.

"I can give you a security deposit and first and last month's rent." I wanted this place. I knew it before I got out of the car. I grew up in a town of two-story colonials with lush lawns and painted shutters. It was a marked change from the neighborhood I now wanted to live in. But this was the new me. 'Sedona me.' 'Please,' I begged silently. 'I want this.' When I get anxious, you can't shut me up. I pressed on.

"I have furniture back east. One phone call and it will be on its way. I'll take good care of your home. I don't smoke, I'm quiet. No wild parties," I ended. *Please, I promise I'll be good.*

"Okay, you're a college professor, right? Are you planning on applying at the University? I know some folks up in Flagstaff." *Yikes.* Seconds ago, he wasn't sure if I was fit to live in his guest home and now, he's offering to help me find a job.

"Oh, no," I protested. "I got a nice severance from my last job and I have some savings. I'll be fine for a while until I figure out my next move. Career move." I added quickly after seeing his reaction. "I'm happy to sign a lease if you want. I'm planning on sticking around."

"Okay," he finally said. "Pay me first and last month and we'll call it a deal. There are still a few days left so let's make it the first of the month officially, but you can start moving in any time." He held out the keys and I reached for my checkbook and a pen. When he told me the monthly rent, I was shocked. It was much less than what I paid for my apartment back home and Sedona was known to be pricey. It was only about half of the amounts listed for the units on Craigslist, and although I hadn't gone inside any of them, I just knew this was much nicer. I wondered if Rick had really laid it on thick about the state of my finances and my stellar character. I certainly hadn't told him about my rainy day fund and I wasn't sure when or if I would. Money can be a touchy subject, especially between men and women. Robbie and I had been living together for a few months and were already talking marriage when I told him just how much the sales of my parents' business and my family home had netted me. He whistled appreciatively.

"God Jax, you really are the total package. Gorgeous, hot, brainy *and* loaded." I smacked him playfully.

"You forgot sweet and funny," I told him.

"And great in bed," he leered suggestively. The afternoon slipped away from us as it so often did, and it wasn't until it was time to make an offer on the house, that the subject of my sizable nest egg came up again. I had argued that a large down payment was the way to go.

"I want to make my money work for us, our money, I mean," I told him. "I'm investing in us, Robbie. It'll keep our monthly payments lower and it's just smart. It's a good investment." He finally agreed, but insisted on making the mortgage payments out of his checking account each month. We had never gotten around to opening a joint account. His salary was way more than mine, but he had virtually no savings when we first got together.

I freaked when Suze suggested I get him to sign a prenup.

"No way," I roared. "He's not like that. I'm not a Kardashian, for Christ's sake."

"You just have to protect yourself, Jax." Suze countered. "I'm sorry to say it, but you hear about this every day. Some rich woman gets duped by some con man." I was livid.

"I mean it, Suze. Stop right now. First off, he's not a gold digger. If you had seen his reaction when he found out about my money, you would know that. And by the way, stories like that are only on trashy daytime TV. You're so quick to judge. Get a life, why don't you?" *Wow.* Back me into a corner and I could be really mean. Suze had packed on quite a few pounds since college and was very unhappy about it. She had confided in me more than once that stress and fatigue combined had her snacking her on the couch watching TV more than she liked to admit. She glared at me.

"Low blow, Jackie. Screw you and screw your boyfriend."

She stomped off and it was a few days before we spoke again. She showed up at my door with a couple of pints one afternoon after work.

"Truce," she said holding out my favorite flavor. I noticed hers was a fat-free frozen yogurt. *Hmmm.*

"I'm sorry," she said. "I just want you to be careful. I hate to see you get hurt."

"But have you ever seen me happier?" I pleaded. "Trust me on this, please." And she said she would try. We never argued about him again. I guess we agreed to disagree. I trusted Robbie. Totally, and he never let me down. During the 71 months that we held a mortgage together, he paid the principal, interest, and homeowner's insurance from his account on time and without comment. From the considerable proceeds of the sale, he added the original down payment to my share and wouldn't even discuss a compromise.

"I let you down, Jax. You invested in us and I blew it. It's your money, it always was." Poor Robbie. He thought he was like his father, when nothing could be less true. It broke my heart that he blamed himself for our split. Even after we resumed the physical aspects of our relationship in bed each Saturday, he remained convinced that the divorce had been his fault. He got that far-away-Robbie look whenever a reminder of our marriage would surface. Unlike most divorced couples, we didn't blame each other. Far from it. We each maintained total responsibility for the demise of our marriage. As if by some unspoken agreement, we rarely 'went there.' Never played the 'if only' game.

"He likes the no-problem side of me," I moaned to Suze in the months after our split. "I can't confide in him the way I used to. I hold back on anything that's difficult or messy." By now Suze knew that in matters of the heart, the only acceptable reaction was to nod her head and shrug her shoulders.

"I know," she would say. But even though she didn't, she would hold my hand when I cried and hugged me when I was inconsolable about the breakup of my marriage.

So, here I was in Sedona less than two years later. I wrote out a check to Edward, thus securing my new place in the sun. I called the moving company holding my things in storage and scheduled a delivery date. Then? What else? It was time to shop. I invested in new towels, sheets, throw pillows, everyday dishes and flatware, and a couple of lamps and a new bedside night table. Just one. I found some cool barstools and a multicolored rug that would tie everything together. Suze sent me a wall plaque proclaiming 'I don't need to flirt. I will seduce you with my awkwardness.' Kind of random, no? I hung it in my kitchen.

When my furniture arrived several days later, Rick showed up and helped me to settle in. I treated him and the movers to pizza and beer. When they all trooped off, I had hoped that Rick would stay for a while. But he said he had to run, so I puttered around that night and I slept in my old bed with its new comforter and sheets. I woke up marveling at the elegant boho-chic environment I had created. It was warm and cozy and I settled in happily. I started going for walks around my new neighborhood and found a number of spots to stop for coffee or some interesting accessory for my new home. I was looking forward to meeting new people and hoped to get to know Rick better as well. A lot better, if you catch my drift. I was determined to make this move work. Failure? Not an option.

CHAPTER 11

♫ It's Aloha Friday ♫

It was Friday. More specifically, it was late afternoon on a Friday. I had been hoping Rick would suggest getting together but despite compulsively checking my phone for a missed call or a text all day, I had not heard from him. The week had started out promising enough. We had met for a drink on Monday night when he finished his shift. It was a noisy, happy hour kind of place, not in the least bit conducive for a romantic get-together, but we managed to find a small table in the corner. Meaningful conversation was a bit of a challenge, but we had a few laughs and shared a plate of nachos. Afterwards he walked me to my car and our good night kiss got pretty steamy. I thought things might get even more interesting, but he left me high and dry, promising to be in touch. I drove home frustrated and proceeded to purge my closet of my frumpy tops and sweaters and vowed to replace them with sexier outfits. *Maybe I wasn't putting out the right vibes?* Maybe he thought I was content to stay in the 'friend zone' forever? I would have to take serious action if this relationship was ever going to heat up.

Those first two weeks, I was pretty busy unpacking and exploring my new neighborhood, but I wasn't used to spending so much time alone. I didn't exactly miss work, but I craved companionship and my daily calls with Suze just weren't enough. I was happy when Rick suggested lunch that Wednesday, but it hadn't worked out too well. A co-worker's Jeep overheated out in the desert and Rick had to head back out to rescue the stranded tourists. I didn't see his text message, so I waited nearly an hour for him and wondered if I had been stood up. When he finally showed up, hot and glistening with sweat (*yikes*) he only had time to gulp down a large iced tea before he had to head back for another scheduled tour. I walked home feeling quite sorry for myself and proceeded to drown my sorrows with a pint of ice cream and a large bowl of microwaved popcorn. And that was my week.

So there I was, alone in a strange town on a Friday night. I had decided that I would kick off the weekend in style. It was a tradition after all. Growing up, I didn't experience much in the way of holiday celebrations. Usually corned beef sometime around the middle of March, ham on Easter, and turkey on Thanksgiving. Oh, and burgers on the Fourth of July. Yes, holidays and meat products were forever linked in my brain. My parents didn't get too involved with holiday decorations and all. They worked a zillion hours a week, or so it seemed. Not a lot of energy for staging elaborate holiday celebrations.

But we did have a tradition that in our own way brought us together just about every Friday night ever since I could remember.

"It's Aloha Friday," my dad would sing off-key as he headed out early for work. My parents made every effort to close the office early on Fridays. They were generally home by five pm; the night was young and full of possibilities. I would run to the drawer in the kitchen and grab the battered, dog-eared folder (appropriately labeled 'Aloha Friday'). It contained take-out menus featuring just about every type of food possible. Our town was not a big one, but it was a college town and that made all the difference. Chinese, pizza, subs (grinders for you folks from Connecticut), but wait there's more: Sushi, Korean barbecue, Italian, Mexican.

Back then, it was usually my mother who made the final decision and intervened when dad and I were in a hopeless cuisine deadlock. The only rule for Aloha Fridays was that we ordered from just one place each week, and gave an outrageous tip to the lucky delivery boy who pulled in our driveway that night.

My dad was the only one who took the Aloha theme literally. Every Friday night, he would emerge from the huge walk-in closet that my parents shared, sporting one of the garish Hawaiian print shirts from his vast collection. Years later, when I was organizing things to donate after I sold their house, those shirts were what did me in. I was systematically sorting his suits and ties with no problem. Zero emotion. When I got to those shirts, however, I lost it. Curled up sobbing on the closet floor in a Hawaiian pile of memories, I was stricken with grief at his early passing but laughing out loud at the wonderful, dear memories I had of my dad. My conservative CPA, starched-collar father, bopping around the kitchen with a spring roll or keeping time with a chicken wing to the rock 'n' roll music emanating from speakers strategically placed around the house, pretending to look for something as he doled out the food.

"Where's the meat and potatoes?" he would shout in his best Irish brogue. Wearing a big grin and a shirt emblazoned with palm trees and hula girls, Tom Sullivan was in his element, enjoying the fruits of his labors with the two loves of his life, my mom and rock 'n' roll. You thought I would say *me,* right? Here we go again. He loved me, okay? On Friday nights, he actually seemed to enjoy my company as well. But it was my mom, blue-eyed Anne Brennan, who stole his heart nearly twenty years before I came along. It's okay. I'm fine with that.

While waiting for the food, my dad's attention turned to music, specifically rock 'n' roll music. His music collection was legendary as was his knowledge of the artists, the bands, and the music 'scene' (his term not mine). I still have most of his music collection, which evolved over the years from vinyl to cassettes to CD's. A purist, he claims to have been disdainful of the short-lived eight-track phase and never caved. Aloha Fridays provided an opportunity for dad to play DJ for his adoring fans- my mom and me. We would make requests, which he would consider, but reject if they didn't fit the theme of the evening. The theme was a moving target and defied logic in anyone's mind but his. He preferred the lesser-known songs and eschewed many of the commercial hits, but he played it all. The Beatles, The Stones, Sly and the Family Stone, Credence, and the Allman Brothers were regulars. He judged the Doors, Jimi Hendrix, and Elvis as overrated and that was the end of the subject.

Once in a while, a friend of mine would join us, but we three were a tight-knit group and really hard to penetrate. I rarely invited anyone back a second time. I asked a high school boyfriend to join us one ill-fated night. *Big mistake.* For the first time ever, my dad was an embarrassment to me. Beating on an imaginary drum set with his fingers or chopsticks or the aforementioned spring roll, was he always such a know-it-all? Did it sound like he was bragging about his knowledge of music? Who cared how a band got together or broke up? Well, he did. And usually, so did I. I ended that night early. At the door, I got a sloppy wet kiss, followed by a whispered, "Boy, your dad is weird," with a shake of his head. I retreated to my room and wallowed. What a freak I was. What a loser. Staying home with my odd couple parents on a Friday night when everyone my age was out driving too fast, getting to third base and doing things that would be talked about in the halls on Monday. Not me—I was singing and dancing with my classic rock parents and stuffing my face on Moo shu and cold sesame noodles. Hmmm ... there had to be some left, no? I had barely eaten that night, suffused with embarrassment as I was. Since we had a guest, Mom had ordered twice as much food as usual. Curious and starving, I slunk down the stairs and hightailed it to the kitchen. I grabbed a plate, loaded it up with all of the delicacies I had missed earlier, and joined my folks on the couch. It was Eric Clapton night after all. It was Aloha Friday. It was good.

Years later, I knew Robbie was the one for me when very early in our relationship, I broached the idea of an evening in. He brought pizza (*amateur!*) and I assembled a collection of CDs that I thought he would enjoy. Early on that first Friday evening, I shared memories of my family tradition with my new boyfriend. He got it, Robbie did.

"Great food and rock 'n roll? That's awesome. An evening with Jackie Sullivan? What could be better?" The guy had style you know? For years we had our own version of Aloha Fridays: Colby—Sullivan style. Robbie and I carried on the tradition following the formula laid down by my dad decades earlier. But that first Friday as a new couple, we started a new weekly tradition: ending the evening in the bedroom or sometimes on the living room floor. Rug burn, tangled sheets, discarded clothing, candles burned down to the quick … Alohaaaaa Friday indeed.

Okay, a few quick confessions. It was only our third date on that first Friday. Hey don't judge me—when you know, you know. Oh, and several of my dad's shirts that I had held onto eventually ended up on Robbie's side of the closet. It's not creepy and I made sure he took them off before we would get too hot and heavy on those Friday nights. Trust me, he in no way resembled my dad, except maybe in coloring and height and overall build. And the candles burning down? Oh please, this is me we're talking about. I would no sooner sleep, let alone even lounge about, with candles still burning. I would disentangle my naked self from Robbie's sleepy embrace, hop up, and snuff them out completely. I couldn't have slept otherwise, sex-sated or not.

But that was then and this was now. It was time to get busy, so I placed my pizza order that first Friday night in my new home in Sedona. Worst pizza ever, I would soon discover. I found better options over the next several weeks. But that night, even lousy pizza tasted like ambrosia to me. After all it was Southern rock night chez Sullivan. Get out your lighters … *Free Bird!*

CHAPTER 12

♫ I Heard it Through the Grapevine ♫

I t wasn't long before I felt like I had settled into the guest house. It was about the same amount of living space as I was used to, so my furniture fit and I guess I did as well. Despite a small kitchen, my new home offered plenty of countertop space, most of which I kept blissfully free of knick-knacks and small appliances. Just a coffee maker, for the most part. You can always tell how I'm doing by checking out my counters. Most days, they're clutter-free and wiped clean. But during times of stress or emotional upheaval? Forget about it. Whenever Suze would stop by, without my saying a word, she would know whether or not I was struggling. Countertops are really a metaphor for life when you think about it. Lately, there were no signs of a struggle. Clutter-free. I should take a picture to text to Suze so she could stop worrying about me.

And my landlord? A nice enough kind of guy. Not the type to invite me in for an iced tea after a long day, but an okay sort. He would probably be willing to sign for my packages, if I got any. Maybe I could even ask him to wait for the cable guy. He didn't seem old enough to be retired, but he was around an awful lot. Not in a creeper kind of way, just whenever I pulled into the driveway and parked under the carport reserved for me, his car was almost always there. He didn't seem lonely or anything. I don't know, maybe he was an artist or an online sex therapist. Who knew? Sedona was full of people with hidden talents and hidden pasts. The barista who concocted my lattes at a nearby café used to be a high school principal back East. Can you imagine? After one too many school board meetings and way too many talks with teachers who were being laid off, she decided to chuck it all and make coffee for a living. But she seemed happy and didn't seem to have too many regrets. I know, because I asked her,

"Do you have any regrets?"

And she said, "Not really."

I liked living there. It was an unseasonably cool summer, rarely made it into the mid-80's, and that was fine with me. And it was a dry heat, not like the humid summers I was used to back east. "My hair doesn't frizz," I would marvel to Suze over the phone. I imagined that it could get pretty hot in the guesthouse without air conditioning, but I would deal with it when the time came. That was East-Coast-Jax, worrying about things like that. Sedona-Jax was ready to roll with the punches, take it one day at a time. 'Chillax' as my students would say. Or as I imagined they might have said. I have actually never heard anyone say that out loud. Until me, just now.

Other things you will never hear me say? 'It's all good.' What does that even mean? All good, everything in the world is good? Honestly. Also, you'll never hear me say; "Now that's what I'm talking about." It's just so cliché. Also, "Ciao." Please, really? I do say literally, a lot. I mean, literally, I say it all the time. It's not in the least bit precise. I mean, I'm not literally starving, not really. Nor am I literally exhausted or literally up to my eyeballs in grading. Except that one time … I also will never be quoted as saying "Be that as it may." I wouldn't even know how to work it in. I also dislike "Fake it 'til you make it." First off, I don't believe that's a good plan and second, I've heard it used way too many times. And nix to "Not on my watch." And to "Nix" as well. I also never use sports analogies. I don't understand them and I'm always messing them up. Also, "Go big or go home." Not from these lips.

I had been living in my new home for about a week when I heard a knock on the door. More of a tap. I almost missed it. It was late in the afternoon. I had been reading and thinking about making some tea, when I heard someone at my door. I wasn't expecting anyone, but that's okay. Sedona-Jax was game. By the time I opened the door and looked out, Edward was already heading halfway across the patio.

"Hey," I called to his retreating form. "Did you need something?"

"Oh, yeah. I thought you had gone out."

"No, I'm here. What's up? Can I do anything for you?" He looked embarrassed.

"No, I was just wondering if you wanted to join me for a drink." Apparently, he *was* the kind of guy to offer a cold drink at the end of a long day. I was wrong.

"Um, sure, yeah okay. When?"

"Well now, I guess, if that's okay."

"Sure, let me just grab some shoes." I found my flip-flops and followed him out my front door and across the brick patio to his back door. We had never exchanged much more than a 'hello' and general pleasantries when we met in the driveway. To be honest, I was getting a bit tired of all that solitude. I mean, we're social beings after all. Need to mingle. So now I was going to have a friendly drink with my landlord. Cool!

I had never been in the big house before. The main living area was even larger than I had imagined. Open floor plan, tons of light, green plants everywhere. And, oh my, two little creatures of the feline variety.

"Oh my God, how cute," I shrieked when I spotted them. Two full-grown Siamese cats, sleek and gorgeous, circled around Edward's legs, eyeing me warily. I knelt down, held out my hand and made what I thought were little tsking sounds guaranteed to draw the little darlings to me. Not going to happen. They backed away from me moving in perfect synchronization. Like they had rehearsed it. Retreating to a sunny corner of the large room, they commenced grooming themselves and each other and ignored us completely.

"They're shy around strangers," said Edward. Shy? No. Disapproving, disdainful, disinterested? Yes.

"What are their names?" I asked.

"Boris and Natasha," replied Edward rather sheepishly.

"Oh, like in the Rocky and Bullwinkle comics."

"Yes." Edward seemed pleased. *Hey, I know my comics.* Yes, I do.

"How old are they; how long have you had them?" I was thrilled. I never got to have a pet growing up. My mother always claimed allergies whenever I clamored for a companion. Not even a hamster or parakeet. Once I brought home Goldie, the class guinea pig for the weekend. I was in fifth grade and had finally worn my mother down. Everyone in the class took turns with Goldie and I was determined that I would have mine. When that Friday afternoon finally came, I was beside myself with joy. At last, something to love. To care for. All mine.

By Saturday morning, I was bored silly. Watching Goldie scamper around, eat, and sleep was thrilling for about an hour. I was not allowed to free her from her cage. My mother made me promise. Our only physical contact came when I stuck my finger through the cage. Goldie's little pink nose sniffed it and for second, we were connected. Then it was over. Shortly thereafter, total boredom set in. I pretty much ignored my little houseguest for the rest of the weekend. I fed her and cleaned her cage and provided her with a fresh newspaper carpet, but I was more than ready on Monday morning to relinquish guardianship. I never volunteered to bring her home again. Not that I really had the chance. When Jack Mills brought her home for the weekend several weeks later, poor Goldie was traumatized by Jack's German Shepherd. When the dog charged Goldie's cage and started barking, it was just too much. The little guinea pig was literally scared to death and collapsed in her cage. Jack swears that he tried to resuscitate Goldie, which resulted in him being teased mercilessly about French kissing a rodent. *Come on, we were twelve.* How do you think we would've handled it? Oh, and he swore that he gave her a proper burial. But I'm certain that Goldie was pronounced dead, wrapped up in newspaper and thrown in the trash, followed by a trip to McDonald's for Jack and a brief discussion about how life is precious and you had to make the most of it ... Blah, blah, blah. I'm a bit of a cynic, I know. If I only had been allowed to have a pet.

Robbie and I approached pet ownership in a manner similar to that of having a baby. Which is to say, we were both for it in theory, but at different times and with varying degrees of enthusiasm. Needless to say, we never took that step, made that leap. It was just never the right time. Something else always seemed to take priority ... an upcoming trip, a project at work. Whatever. It was just as well, because joint custody of a beagle was too weird to imagine, even for me.

Now I would have two gorgeous cats living right next door.

"Oh, they're beautiful. Which one is which? Oh look, I think they're getting used to me." The slightly larger one was Natasha. Boris was little smaller, but sturdier. Both were gorgeous specimens. Seal point Siamese with brilliant blue eyes. Boris' were slightly crossed, but only if you looked closely. Natasha didn't seem to mind. Bored with being gawked at and immune to the unending stream of baby talk I was spewing, Natasha continued to groom herself while Boris curled up against the sofa, and with his back to me, promptly indulged in a catnap. Such is my impact on the male of the species.

Edward ushered me out onto the deck that ran along the side of the house. It was beautifully appointed with several chaise lounges, a grill the size of most cars, and a view that was undeniably the most beautiful I've ever seen.

"Oh my God, it's gorgeous," I cried. I was mesmerized and overcome with the beauty I was facing. "Do you ever get sick of this, ever take it for granted?" I asked. *Please say no!*

"No, never, "he replied. We stood side by side for a few moments lost in the view of the red rocks contrasted against bright blue skies. This is what I came to Sedona for. Sure, believe that.

Edward interrupted my thoughts by offering me a beer. I gratefully accepted. Not much of a beer drinker, but when in Rome, plus it would give me something to do with my hands. Take me out of my comfort zone and I fold like a rug. I offered to help, but he assured me that he was fine and bustled away. I indulged my senses for a few more moments then stretched out on an overstuffed chaise. When he returned, he was balancing a tray containing two bottles of beer, a bowl of still steaming microwave popcorn, and a stack of cocktail napkins proclaiming 'It's five o'clock somewhere.' Touched by his thoughtfulness, I toasted our continued good health and my happiness with both the view and the company. We clinked bottles and I proceeded to burn the roof of my mouth with scalding popcorn. Happy hour!

Over the next couple of hours, I nursed my beer and devoured the popcorn while Edward enjoyed two more beers and told me the story of his life. Really. Didn't hold back. I learned that he had been born in New Jersey, the third child and only son, two older sisters, and two younger sisters. He was named after his paternal grandfather. It was always Edward, not Ed, never Eddie. But 'Coop' was okay, I guess. That's how Rick had referred to him.

With a degree in business from Rutgers University, Coop got an entry-level job in the burgeoning cable TV industry. It was the late 70's and business was booming. Over the next twenty years, he rose through the ranks, jumping from one company to another in increasingly responsible and highly stressful and very lucrative positions. Still in his early 40's, his career peaked as Senior VP of Operations when his company was bought out by a large investment firm, whose only goal was to strip down the organization he had built up and sell off the pieces. Apparently in this case, the whole was worth less than the parts. He was offered a fat severance package and cashed out, retired fifteen years ago at the age of forty-three. Hell, that's only a few years older than I am now. So young to retire. Too young. Had I retired?

The climb to the top had taken a toll on Edward's personal life, and an early marriage had produced a daughter who had to be around thirty or so by now. Never close to her dad, the strained relationship grew even more tenuous when he was married a second time to a much younger woman. Based on what he told me, his second wife would've been close to thirty or so as well. I regarded my landlord with a new found level of interest. A top executive flying all around the country making deals and mergers that made headlines? A father? Husband to a young trophy wife? My bush-pruning, Teva-wearing, more gone than gray landlord? *Coop, you stud!* Once again, I marveled at how people are so much more than they appear. I vowed to avoid snap judgments in the future and promised myself that I would take the time to get to really get to know the people I had regular contact with and stop assuming and judging. Appearances can be deceiving. Still waters run deep. You get my point, right? At any rate, no comment on the status of the second Mrs. Cooper. Had they split up or was she finishing high school? Oh, that was mean. I would have to find out. Would Rick know?

After the sun went down, and believe me when I tell you it was a marvelous sunset, it got really cool on the deck. Goose bump cool. I shivered and Coop apologized.

"I'm sorry. I've completely monopolized the conversation. I haven't given you a chance to talk. I know next to nothing about you, just your name and the fact that Rick speaks so highly of you." At the sound of his name, I shivered again.

"Oh yeah, Rick. How do you know him?" I asked. Coop was rather vague, I have to say. Apparently, they had mutual friends and ran in the same social circle. Really? Rick and

Edward? But in Sedona, you never knew. Stop judging, ask more questions. Must learn more.

"Is he seeing anyone?" I asked innocently.

"Rick?" Edward chuckled appreciatively "Oh yeah, a lot of someones, it would seem. A real player. I mean not in a bad way or anything. I mean, he's a great guy. Just, just a ladies' man, I guess." *Ooh. Mixed feelings.* I was glad to hear there was no one steady but apprehensive at the thought of competing for his attention. What did I want from Rick or any guy? To get married again? After Robbie, it was doubtful. Been there, done that. If I couldn't have what my folks had, what was the point? But a boyfriend? *God, was I thirteen? Grow up.* A lover, companion, friend with benefits? I wondered what my chances were. Could I attract him? Did he like me like *that*? Was I ready to be one of many? Or should I hold out to be the only one? So many questions. And one from Coop.

"So, are you interested in Rick?" he asked. I blushed and Coop leaned in. I caught a glimpse of an earlier Edward. I suddenly saw signs of the dashing executive who had impressed shareholders and attracted a young bride. His tone became warmer, less teasing.

"He's a great guy, Jackie. Don't get me wrong. I just don't know if …"

"If I'm his type?" I ventured. God, just because I wore sensible shoes and had a low-maintenance hairstyle and rarely remembered to put on makeup … that didn't mean I couldn't be sexy, desirable. Falling for men who were way better looking than me must be my fatal flaw. Coop looked at me, looked me up and down.

"No," he said with just a touch of wistfulness. "You're definitely his type. I'm just not sure if he's yours. I just don't want to see you get hurt," he said, absentmindedly patting my knee.

"I'm a big girl; don't worry about me," I retorted. I was a bit miffed. *Who did this guy think he was anyway?* I barely knew him. Who was he to give me advice about my love life? Realizing he had hurt my feelings, he sat back, then decided to stand up. Alrighty then. The closeness we had built up, the ease of conversation we had enjoyed was gone. It could return again, but for now I decided to take my leave, make my exit.

"Got to go," I said brightly. "Thanks for the beer. Sorry I ate all your popcorn."

"I'm sorry I talked your ear off and for what I said about Rick. What do I know? Two failed marriages. I'm no expert on relationships." Okay—so the young Mrs. Coop was not in the picture. Unless the relationship was anything like Robbie's and mine. One mystery solved. Now, how could I get out of here without any more Rick talk? I had heard enough for one night. I needed to process all this new intel. There was no sign of the cats as we walked through his living room. At the door, he patted my shoulder.

"I'm glad you're here," he said. "I'm glad we're neighbors." I nodded my agreement and told him I would see him around. I thanked him again, then race-walked across the deck and flew into the little guest house. My bladder was bursting for sure, but I really just wanted to be alone. Daily hikes had conditioned me to the point that I was in reasonably good shape but I felt as if I had run an emotional marathon. My breath was ragged and uneven. I leaned against the counter separating my dining area and living space for support. *What had I done?* Thoughts were swirling around in my head. Uprooted my life for some playboy tour guide who could never love me? Never commit? Dejected, I returned from the bathroom and slumped on the couch. I flipped channels for a while before settling on a Meg Ryan romp from the 90's. 'Relax,' I told myself. Take a deep breath.

Deciding to avoid contact with friends on the East Coast, I powered off my cell and closed the lid on my laptop. No chatting with Suze tonight. I sought solitude. I fell asleep on the couch, then dragged myself off to bed when I woke at three am with a stiff neck and a dry mouth. I lay on my back and tried to shut off the thoughts still swirling in my head. Tried to slow my breathing, calm my nerves. I focused on my body, leaving my heart and my mind behind. Gassy from the popcorn, I finally fell into a restless sleep.

If I dreamed, I don't remember, but I woke up several hours later. Strangely rested and mildly optimistic. Coffee, then a hike? Then eggs? Yes. I started my day. Powering my phone up, I saw that Rick had left me a text last evening. Probably while I was hanging with Edward.

"Dinner?" Oh shit, last night? No, he had apparently called at eleven p.m. in advance to ask me out for tonight. Like a real date. Interesting. I texted back. Slowly. Miss Casual.

"Sure, pick me up at 7?"

A few minutes later, he texted back. "In the mood 2 cook. Off at 7. Come over @ 8? I'll text directions later."

"Sounds great. See you then," I texted back. He wanted to cook for me, Chez Rick? *Yikes*. Should I bake a dessert? Get wine? Shave my legs? Yes, yes, and definitely yes!

CHAPTER 13

♫ Night Moves ♫

I found myself humming happily as I tidied up, checked my email and paid a few bills online. I had a date tonight.

'What to wear? I wondered. I didn't want to overdo it or look like I was trying too hard. I finally decided on skinny jeans and a cute top with a pair of sparkly sandals and a light jacket. I considered packing some toiletries but stopped myself. It's just dinner, I reasoned. *But still.*

I was ready to go by late afternoon, but I forced myself to start a new book and killed some time by watching the news and flipping between game shows. Allowing twenty minutes of travel time, I followed the directions that Rick had texted me and arrived at his place just a few minutes past eight.

How can I begin to describe this cabin in the woods? Off the beaten track? Check. Rustic? Check. Charming? Well, to be determined. I parked my car near a beat-up pickup truck that I knew to be Rick's and hopped out. He came outside and seemed really happy to see me. A friendly hug turned into a kiss that quickly escalated to something more. We pulled apart, but I knew that it wouldn't be long before we would be embracing again. Mentally I did a little victory dance.

"God, I'm glad you're here," he said. *God, I'm glad I shaved my legs,* I thought. *Slut.*

"C'mon, I'll show you around." Rick took my hand and led me through the weather-beaten front door. Inside, the cabin was a little more livable than it appeared from the outside. A fire was crackling in the hearth and it felt warm and comforting, compared to the chilly evening air. It also brightened up the rather dim interior.

"Not much natural light," I quipped. The pine trees created a dense overhang and I doubted that sunlight ever penetrated the dark, but somehow not gloomy cabin.

"No, I get enough sun on the job," Rick countered. "I like it dark." The twelve-year-old in me would have responded, "That's what she said," but I resisted the urge.

"Oh, yeah, I'm sure. Lots of sun on the job, right?" *God, I was an idiot.* Why was I so nervous? I looked around as my eyes got used to the relative darkness. The only artwork displayed were a few framed photographs of Sedona sunsets.

"These are nice," I told him. "Did you take them?"

"No" he replied. "A friend did." *Hmmm, a friend.* I saw no TV or radio, no computer. Did he spend evenings in the dark, reading? I saw no books either. *Who was this guy?* Hadn't the Unabomber adopted a similar lifestyle? I accepted his offer of a beer and we sat down on the battered leather sofa that faced the fireplace. A couple of end tables and a rustic coffee table completed the furnishings in the main room. From my vantage point on the couch, I could see a tiny kitchen and a door that I imagined led to his bedroom. *Hold your horses, hot stuff,* I told myself.

We spent a very companionable hour on the couch. I nursed my beer while Rick finished off a couple. I filled him in on what I had been doing for the past week and how I was getting settled into my new home. I thanked him again for the housing referral.

Yeah," he said, shaking his head. "That Coop. What a character. He's something else." I asked him how he knew Coop and he was kind of noncommittal.

"Oh, just around," he said. "Sedona is a small town. You'll see." Rick shared some stories about the challenges and rewards of being a tour guide. One particular story about his colleagues got my full attention.

"So, there's about eighty of us, you know. Pretty even split between girls and guys." The feminist in me bristled at his reference to grown women as 'girls', but I held back. Maybe some of the tour guides were pretty young. *Don't judge*, I reminded myself. He told me about an incident earlier in the week, when one of the girls got the attention of a 4-wheeling Jeep driving tourist up at Broken Arrow. "Rental," he sneered derisively. The young man was apparently turned on or turned off at the site of a mere 'girl' expertly operating the brightly colored Jeep and carrying a load of passengers to boot. Showing off, he tried to pass her while heading up a steep and rather narrow passageway. But his driving skills were apparently no match for young Chrissy's. He spun his tires, slid sideways and ended up in a ditch. Refusing her offer of a tow and now thoroughly pissed-off, he launched into an angry, obscenity-laden tirade about women drivers. Later, he tried to get Chrissy in trouble by reporting her to the tour company. But she had already told her boss what had transpired and every one of her passengers backed up her story, some with video recorded on their phones. Later that evening, the bozo found her profile on Facebook and asked her out on a date.

"They're getting married next month," Rick finished.

"What? Wait, you're kidding, right?"

"Just the last part," Rick chuckled. "He did ask her out, but she never responded. Didn't want to set him off again."

"Yikes," I countered. I know, smooth, huh? How do I come up with all of this sparkling banter?

Rick added, "You meet all kinds, it goes with the job. Yeah, and answering the same questions again and again." Okay, this I could talk about. Back on solid ground for me.

"That must be tough. I know what that's like from being in the classroom," I told him. Rick nodded vigorously.

"Yeah, I have a few pat answers that I can always count on. When I'm really beat or just burned out from talking, I've found that one of these will always work: 'Just around the bend,' 'About ten minutes or so,' and 'In about a mile.' Always works."

"Me too," I responded excitedly. "I've got those too. 'It's on the syllabus,' 'Yes, it'll be on the test,' and 'Next class for sure.'"

"Who would ever think we'd have so much in common," Rick teased. "A big-time college professor and a lowly tour operator."

"Former college professor," I reminded him. I didn't want to get into how I was going to manage without a paycheck or what my plans were, so I switched gears. Back to his job.

"The driving looks hard," I suggested.

"Oh yeah, crazy motor skills required," he laughed. "Not to mention nerves of steel and you've got to be strong like bull." He flexed his biceps at me and winked playfully. I laughed out loud. Oh God, what a flirt. Him, not me. I was in trouble. Big trouble. Good trouble. Conversation slowed down after that and a bit of snuggling led to kissing, then a full on make out session. He half carried me, half dragged me (willingly, I might add. I went willingly) through the door into his bedroom. I had been correct about the door. We crash landed onto a neatly made double bed and proceeded to get to know each other. Really well. Later, we sat on the kitchen floor and devoured the pasta that Rick had prepared for our dinner. I haven't had a lot of experience with this sort of thing, so I wasn't certain if I was expected to stay over or not. I assumed we would spend what was left of the night together, when he found me a T shirt of his to sleep in. I finger brushed my teeth with the chalky organic toothpaste I found near the sink and joined him in bed. We drifted off and after a few hours of sleep, Rick was refreshed and raring to go (to work), but I felt kind of spacey and sluggish. He scrambled eggs and I made toast with the twelve-grain bread I found on the counter. We washed it all down with organic apple juice, although I was wishing for coffee. My brownies forgotten, I drove home through the early dawn light while Rick showered and got ready for his first tour of the day. Before I left, he kissed me lightly on the lips and said, "Talk to you later." The old me would have panicked at the lack of a follow-up date.

Would he call me? When? Was I just a one-night stand? But I was either too tired or too relaxed to care right then. Whatever.

"Sounds good, see you Rick," I said casually, waved and drove off. No strings attached, I thought. I'm so modern. I didn't make a single false turn as I maneuvered my way through the pitch-dark mountain roads leading to town. As if on autopilot, I drove through the quiet streets of uptown Sedona that would be teeming with tourists and locals alike in just a few hours. As I pulled into my driveway, my thoughts were on sleep, followed by a hot shower, and a trough of coffee.

Okay, I had done what I set out to do. He likes me, he really likes me, I thought. This was good. I was happy, right? Maybe. *Hmmm*. Call Suze. After the shower, while drinking the coffee. Suze would know. Her straightforward approach to life's challenges and a dose of her no-nonsense advice was just what I needed. But first things first. Need sleep. What a magnificent sunrise, I thought to myself as I crossed the patio and let myself in. I could get used to this.

CHAPTER 14

♫ Moves Like Jagger ♫

I was early. Just a few minutes, but he wasn't there yet. I looked around as I sat down and started to sip my coffee. I had been seeing him nearly every day right around this time. I know he saw me. I could feel him looking at me as I sat in the bright morning sunshine and enjoyed my coffee. He was always alone. He appeared to prefer it. But he always watched me. Curious and a bit wary. I wondered daily what would happen, if I made a move. Approached him. Tried to pick him up. I was afraid I would scare him off. So, I sat here every day and drank my coffee. After a while, he would take his leave. Stroll away as if he had something important to tend to. More like a strut. He probably had someone. Someone who loved him. Then why is he here every day looking at me? If he has it so good at home, what does he want from me?

Oh, he was here. Out of the corner of my eye I spotted him sauntering along just as casual as you please. Not a care in the world. He sat in his usual spot about twenty yards from me. So, there we were once again. Should I make the first move?

Languidly he scratched his ear and began to groom himself, his long tail swishing back and forth. Wait, you know he's a cat, don't you? What, you thought it was a guy? Of course. Just what I need is another man in my life. I have an ex whose memory seems to grow ever fonder despite the distance, or was it because of the distance? A new lover who is as casual and hard to read as my feline friend here. Oh, and a kindly landlord who was becoming more friendly by the day. It was actually nice having someone looking out for me, bringing me fresh basil from his garden, inviting me over for a beer and a chance to gape at his beautiful view at sunset. No, I had enough male companionship for now.

But a cat? That could be fun. I decided to make my move. It was now or never. I fished the Ziploc baggie I had brought from my pocket. I dumped the contents onto a napkin and put it down on the ground, several feet away in his direction. Then I waited. I didn't have to wait long. Curiosity and hunger got the best of him. Casually, he sauntered over, stopping a couple of times to lick himself. His coat was shiny and not in the least bit matted. If he was a stray, he hadn't been one for long. If a house pet, his humans had failed to provide him with a collar or any type of visible identification. Up close, he was even more handsome that I had thought. A brown and gray tiger, he had an extremely long tail and a pair of bright green eyes. Arriving at the snack I laid out for him, he took one more lick with his paw and glanced in my direction. Not wanting him to know I was watching, I adjusted my sunglasses and pretended to examine my coffee mug. Assured of his privacy, he proceeded to devour the mound of chopped up chicken I had prepared. He was hungry and I noticed his ribs were quite prominent now that he was closer to me. Satisfied that he had lapped up every last bite, he sat back and licked his lips. If he was a human, he might've belched or loosened his belt.

Satisfied and with a full belly, my new friend circled round and round and stretched out on the ground only a few feet from me. Content in the sun, he dozed for an hour so. I sat watching him the whole time. Sedona-Jax was getting good at being in the moment. I had all of the time in the world.

Eventually he got up, arched his back, stretched, and without so much as a glance in my direction, he sauntered away, through the backyard and then disappeared under some bushes. *What a cool cat*, I marveled.

The next day, I would put out more chicken and maybe a saucer of milk. I would get to my spot in the backyard even earlier and lay out his meal a little closer to me. At this rate, it would take all week to win him over. But so what? I have the time. I could be patient as long as we ended up together. I poured out the remainder of my now tepid coffee into the grass, gathered up the moist napkin and walked toward the house in search of more caffeine and a long hot shower. Would Coop mind if I had a pet? How would Boris and Natasha feel? Would my pet stay inside or would our relationship stall at the 'I feed him and he comes and goes as he pleases' stage? I voted for inside with an occasional night off to prowl. But a collar and ID tag? Yes, that was nonnegotiable. That was a deal-breaker. I wanted everyone to know that I belonged to him. At least I figured it was a him. I would name my new pet Jagger either way. I have been adopted. Meoww!

CHAPTER 15

♫ What I Need is a Good Defense ♫

"You should've told me." Robbie's tone was harsh and got my immediate attention. His message was crystal clear and I was instantly awake and on high alert. I knew what he was pissed off about. I had some 'splainin' to do. But this is me. I tried to stall for time.

"What? I don't know …"

"Forget it, Jax. You know exactly what I mean. C'mon. You should've told me yourself." Okay the jig was up. It was time to come clean. I'm ready to have this conversation, right? Well … almost.

"I have no idea what you're talking about, Robbie, and it's not even seven am, is it?" I rolled over on my side to confirm the time. Yes 6:40 am. Two hours later on the East Coast, he had had more time to prepare and at least a couple of coffees. And the element of surprise was in his favor. I was doomed.

"You didn't move to Sedona for the red rocks and the blue skies. You moved for him." Once again, faced with no alternative but the truth, I lied.

"Him? What do you mean?" For a split-second Coop and his weathered visage crossed my mind. Huh?

"Rick. The tour guide? Ring any bells?"

"Oh, Rick," I sputtered.

"Are you in love with him?" Love?

"No, of course not. It's not like that. We're just, well, it's complicated, okay?"

"That's not what I heard. Love at first sight, that's what I heard."

"It's not like that," I pressed.

"Yeah, well your secretary tells a different story," he countered.

"Who?"

"Ellen. You know who I mean."

"Oh, the receptionist. She's not really …"

"I don't give a fuck what her job title is. I ran into her at the hardware store. She recognized me. It took me a minute, but by then she's all 'It's so romantic. I just love it. I mean she goes out there for a conference, falls in love, and then loses her job and gets the guy. It's fate, you know.' God, Jackie."

"What were you doing in a hardware store?" I asked curiously. Angrier than I've ever heard him, Robbie fired back at me.

"Who cares? Not the point. Focus, ferchrissakes. I couldn't believe what she was saying, but I played along … all 'oh yeah, really' but I kept thinking, maybe she's talking about someone else, maybe she thinks I'm someone else. Then I heard Jackie and Sedona and I knew. Fuck you."

I mentally took Ellen off my next run of postcards and struggled to come up with something. Some excuse, some defense. I had hurt him deeply. I had nothing.

"I know Rob. You're right. I should've told you." And I should have. All the fight gone, Robbie's voice was now sad, defeated.

"So it's true, really? You're in love with a tour guide?" Wait, was he judging what Rick did for a living? Should I tell him that he was kind of like the assistant manager? Or at least Lead Tour Guide? Did it matter? *Not the point*, I told myself. *Focus.*

"It's not love. Really. We're just friends."

"Friends with benefits, right?" Damn Justin Timberlake for making a movie so memorable that the premise became part of pop culture. Okay, time to get serious. Go on the attack.

"I don't know why you care anyway. We're divorced, remember?" Yeah, take that.

"Okay, you're right. I just don't understand why you told everyone else but kept it from me," he conceded. He had me there.

"I was embarrassed," I pleaded. "It just seemed so weird to tell you. You would've asked me questions and made me think about things that I wasn't ready to think about." I really don't know exactly what I had been feeling. I just knew I had to get away, to start over. "I'm sorry, Rob."

"You should've told me," he responded. "I could've handled it. You should've trusted me."

By now, I was exhausted. Spent. I stopped trying to right all the wrongs, er, alleged wrongs.

"Yeah, you're right, Robbie."

"What?"

"I said you're right. C'mon, you heard me."

"Note the date and time, ladies and gentlemen. Jackie Sullivan has conceded defeat." Okay, now this was getting annoying. Silence was my response.

"So, what's he like?" he asked innocently. I did *not* want to go there.

"I don't know, he's in his mid-thirties, from the Midwest, I guess. Divorced, hikes, into fitness and eating healthy. He's a vegetarian." I added.

"Wow, you must be missing those cheeseburgers," he teased.

"I get plenty of cheeseburgers," I countered. "All the cheeseburgers I want." Wait, were we really still talking about meat here? I'm getting confused.

"So he's younger than you, huh?"

"Really, that's all you heard? Yeah, a few years, I guess. What does that matter?"

"Are you two serious? Exclusive? How does he feel about it? Is he ready to commit, to make it Facebook official?"

"Oh puh-leeze." I responded. I kept my tone light. "We're just taking it slow. Keeping our options open." That was the understatement of the year.

"Well, awesome. I'm happy for you, Jax." I was waiting for a big but.

"But?"

"But nothing. I can't wait to meet him," Robbie continued. What?

"You know, when I visit."

"You're still coming?" I asked weakly.

"Well yeah, sure. Why not? Maybe I'll fall in love with a local gal and quit my job. We could be neighbors. Double date. What do you think?"

"I think you're an asshole." I told him. Okay, time to cut this short. I stood up and stretched.

"Listen, this has been just a slice of heaven, you know? Catching up and all. But I was still asleep and I've got to grab a shower and I need some coffee. Stat."

Before I had driven to Arizona, we had talked about Robbie coming out for a visit, but I really thought it was just talk. To be honest, I missed him. No one had ever loved me like Robbie. Truly. When we were good, we were great. I always felt safe, valued, loved. But here, in Sedona? How would that even work? Would he stay here, with me? What about Rick? We were super casual. But I saw him, a lot. A lot of him. Would they fight over me? Or go for a beer and swap Jax stories? Ugghhh. No, not happening.

"Okay. Well, think about it. Maybe Thanksgiving, but I could get more time off at Christmas."

"Well, yeah, you should come. For sure. Let's talk about it okay? I'll call you when you're sound asleep. Give you a hard time."

"Don't get your panties in a bunch, Jax. I do want to visit. I want to see you, check out Sedona. Maybe take a tour. If you and Rick are playing house by then, I can stay nearby. I wouldn't want to cramp your style."

"Okay, shut up. I want you to visit. It won't be weird, I promise." Oh, it was already weird, but what can you do?

"Go back to sleep. Don't worry. We're fine, yeah?" he asked. I told him we were. We said our goodbyes and I lay back down and pulled the covers over my head. Burrowing in, I realized what I really felt. Relief! Robbie and I had been talking at least a couple of times a week since I had left. I had tried to keep the conversations light, chatty, regaling him with stories of my new place, Jagger, Coop, and my new friend Maureen, the principal-turned-barista. What I saw on my hikes. I just neglected to tell him whom I frequently hiked with or got coffee with or slept with. Okay, I had been holding back and now I could come clean. Come out of the closet, so to speak. Stand tall and proud. I had moved on, met someone else. But it wasn't really like that. Not really. I threw back the covers. Shower, but first start the coffee. Time to get up.

An hour later, I was at it again. Fighting, over the phone. Not my day, I guess. This time with Suze. I had called her to get her view on the subject. I was expecting her to agree that Rob was out of line and that he had no right to be pissed at me. The only problem was, her view was different from mine. And it was the same as Robbie's.

"I can't believe you're agreeing with him. This is unreal," I fumed.

"You should have told him, Jax. Really, you were still sleeping with him. Dating him. You should have told him you were moving on."

"I told him I was moving thousands of miles away, for God's sake. Two time zones. What part of that doesn't say 'moving on?' And we weren't *dating*, for God's sake. What are you, twelve?"

"I'm just saying you should have told him why."

"Crap, can't you just agree with me?" *Honestly, just once.* "Just say 'I know what you mean Jax. He's not being reasonable. You're right and he's wrong.'" *Just fucking agree with me.* Suze was not convinced.

"You should have told him, Jax. Now he knows. So, deal with it. Time to face the music."

"I gotta go," I mumbled. "I'll call you later."

I put the phone down and looked around. Jagger was nowhere to be seen. Feeling like everyone was against me, I pulled on a pair of running shoes and punished myself with a brisk walk, well actually a climb. Coop's property bordered the high desert, just steps from my back door and I could get lost in nature. It still took my breath away. If I craved civilization, I could go out the front of the property and was only a few blocks from a really good deli and the best latte place ever, Caffe-Nation. I had found it and Maureen almost by accident. I was shuffling by and almost missed it: a small sign promising hot coffee, fresh pastries, and no attitude. I like hot coffee, I realized. I like fresh pastry. I was ambivalent about attitude, but two out of three ain't bad. It was a great find. But today, nature called. I pushed myself up and over the large rock formations dotting the landscape and quickly broke a sweat.

Despite the fact that I neglected to apply my usual coating of SPF 50 and had forgotten my wide-brimmed hat, I kept walking, kept climbing. I knew where I was going. Anywhere I couldn't see Robbie's face or hear Suze's voice. They were right. I should have been upfront with Rob. I owed him that much.

Much later, after a shower—a cool one this time—and a liberal amount of aloe vera gel to sooth my burned skin, I decided to try to make amends. Curled up on my couch, I texted Robbie. I told him that I missed him. I didn't say I loved him. But I did. Love him. And I was pretty certain that he knew it. I asked him to call me whenever he felt like talking. I hoped it would be soon.

CHAPTER 16

♫ American Woman ♫

They say you never forget your first time. Whoever 'they' are. But in this case, they're right. It was beautiful and magical and over way too soon. Get your mind out of the gutter, I'm talking about my first Sedona sunset. At least the first sunset viewed from the top of the mountain in the center of town that I had been hearing about since I first arrived. Earlier that evening, Rick had swung by to pick me up.

"You'll love it," he assured me. "Everyone does."

I had dressed casually and at his suggestion, traded in my flip-flops for a sturdy pair of sneakers.

"Not too crowded," Rick observed as we parked on the side of the street. "Good. Let's get going. We want to make sure to get a prime spot for your first time." He took my hand as we crossed the surface street and began our ascent.

"It's all about foot placement," Rick assured me. "Be careful and pay attention. You have to know where your next move is coming from." Always the tour guide. Three weeks of daily hikes had more than prepared me for that evening.

After we made it to the top of the huge rock formation, I got to look around. What a sight. 360° of sheer beauty. It was a bright, clear evening and Rick assured me that the conditions were right for a perfect sunset. He was correct. It was spectacular. At first, I fiddled around with my phone, taking shots and trying to shoot some video. I finally gave up my efforts to capture the evening on film, opting to be more in the moment and rely on my senses instead. Rick was sitting cross legged on the rock directly facing the rapidly setting sun. I started to kneel down next to him when he pulled me onto his lap. Thrilled, I snuggled in against him and delighted in how tiny and fragile I felt, yet strong and fearless at the same time. I was able to relax totally, which is no small feat for me, and just enjoy the show. Almost as quickly as it began, it was over and only the promise of the best pizza ever got me up and moving.

"So what did you think?" Rick asked as we drove through town.

"It was spectacular," I told him. "Thank you, I loved it." And I did. I was happy. Life was good. Being with Rick was easy. Super easy. I enjoyed his company and we clearly had the right chemistry. If our conversations were a tad light on depth, well, that was okay. He was gorgeous and sweet and while not overly demonstrative, he put a lot of thought into making sure that I was experiencing all of the things that made desert living so special. After a delicious pizza (half mushroom for him and half pepperoni for me), we ended up back at my place. Unwilling to share me, Jagger clamored to be let out almost as soon as we got there. I have to admit, he wasn't a fan. I mean, my new cat didn't seem to approve of my new boyfriend. More of a dog person at heart, Rick didn't seem to notice that he was being dissed. We settled on the couch and Rick took control of the remote.

"Are there any channels you don't get?" he marveled as he flicked through seemingly hundreds of different options for our viewing pleasure. I shrugged noncommittally.

"It's Coop," I told him. "I'm just another TV set on his account. I get what he gets." Apparently, part of Coop's golden parachute package included free cable for life or something. I mean who really needs 500 channels?

We settled on an action-adventure flick that had to be at least ten years old, yet Rick was immediately absorbed. It just wasn't grabbing my attention and besides, I wanted to talk. And no, I didn't start out by saying "We need to talk." We're not there yet on the relationship spectrum. I doubted we ever would be. To tell you the truth, Rick sometimes got on my nerves. I admit to being a bit of a snob sometimes, okay, but he actually said things like, "for all intensive purposes." Once he conceded that something was a *mute* point. C'mon. Really?

And he chewed funny, too. It was mildly irritating, especially in the morning. We were low-maintenance, zero drama, no games. Just friends, who on occasion got extremely friendly. But still.

"So can you even get TV reception out where you live?" I asked him. Rick shrugged.

"I don't know. I doubt it. To tell you the truth, I've never checked." And immediately gave his full attention back to the TV screen.

But I wanted to find out more about this man with whom I had been spending a fair amount of time. What made him tick? How did he spend his days off? What did he do with his evenings, with no music, no TV, no Internet, no books?

"So do you miss it?" I asked him.

"Miss what?" he asked warily.

"You know. TV, mass media, civilization." He laughed.

Gail Ward Olmsted

"Oh sure, sometimes. But if that's the price I have to pay for getting to live where I do, then it's worth it."

"But, how do you spend your time?" I pressed.

"I get by," Rick told me. "With a little help from my friends," he added. *Hmmm*. Again with the friends. Never overly perceptive, I think he knew that I still wasn't satisfied. He knew I wanted more. Maybe it was my body language. I uncrossed my arms and sat back on the couch. All in good time.

"No really," he said. "During the season, I work sixty to seventy hours a week. When it's slow during the winter, I usually take a second job."

"Really?" I asked incredulously. "What do you do?"

"It depends. I know a guy who owns a restaurant over in Cottonwood. I take over for him, usually after the holidays. It gives him a chance to visit family back East. Sometimes I tend bar, other times I work in the kitchen. Whatever needs to be done," he concluded.

"You're a man of many talents," I marveled.

"You don't know the half of it," Rick continued. "I've refinished hardwood floors, remodeled kitchens, even helped Coop get this place ready." I looked around at my beautifully appointed living quarters in awe.

"Wait, you're kidding me, right? You built this place?"

"Well, I had help," Rick said easily. "Coop was hoping that his daughter would stay for a while, so I helped him get the place in shape."

"He doesn't say much about her," I said. "She's grown, right? I mean like our age, yeah?"

"Well, maybe my age," Rick teased me.

"Just how old do you think I am, anyway?" I asked him. My spidey senses tingling, I had always assumed he was just a few years younger than I was, but the subject had never come up. Rick sat back and looked suspicious.

"That's a trick question, right? My ex used to ask 'do these pants make me look fat?' No matter how I answered I was in trouble. If I said 'yeah, kind of,' well that wouldn't work. But if I said 'no,' the next question would be something like 'so do I usually look fat?' Either way, I was screwed. A no-win situation."

As much as I would have liked to hear more about the ex-wife he rarely mentioned, I had to know.

"Oh c'mon. You can tell me," I assured him "Age means nothing to me." He looked at me closely. Suddenly self-conscious, I prayed silently that he would be kind.

"I don't know," he said, "maybe 40's? 40-ish," he amended quickly when he saw my horrified reaction.

"I'm thirty-nine." I told him. "Thirty-nine, not quite forty." *Damn.* "So does that make me a cougar?" I questioned him. *Be careful how you answer this one. You're on some pretty thin ice, mister. Tonight's sleepover lies in the balance.* And by the way, I really hate the term "cougar." I mean, what do they call older guys who hook up with younger women? Besides lucky that is.

"No way," he assured me, "I'm thirty-three. To be a cougar, I'd have to be at least ten years younger or you would have to be ten years older," he said, trying to keep a straight face. Now he's a comedian. Wow ... thirty-three, I thought. If I had babysat in my teen years, like most of my friends did, I could've been paid for watching him. Supervised his potty training. Changed his diapers. *Gross.* Erase that pervy image. Enough talking for one night. We finished watching the movie, started making out during the eleven o'clock news and ended up in bed. Much later, I lay awake listening for Jagger. I guessed he was pulling an all-nighter, since I had an overnight guest.

I eventually fell asleep and woke hours later with bright sunshine streaming in. Showered and rested and looking way too good even wearing his clothes from the night before, Rick came in to say goodbye. Oddly, I thought about Robbie. How he would bring me coffee in the morning. Even when things started to go bad between us, coffee served in bed was a constant.

"Coffee?" I asked hopefully.

"Never touch the stuff," Rick assured me. "Gotta run." A quick peck on the top of my head and he was gone. He let himself out and I decided to stay a few more minutes in bed. I had just burrowed back into a comfortable position, when Jagger jumped up beside me.

"Oh, there you are," I chided him gently." Were you waiting for Rick to leave?" In response, my feline room-mate circled a few times and settled in down near my feet. With one paw on my ankle, my little night owl settled into a deep sleep.

"You've convinced me," I told him and happily joined him in slumber. After a couple of hours of shuteye, I took a long shower and decided to treat myself to breakfast out. Leaving my sleeping kitty and thinking of nothing more than what kind of muffins Mo would have on display that morning, I headed out into the bright sunshine towards town. It was not a long walk, maybe ten or fifteen minutes, if I kept to a brisk pace, but I had no reason to hurry. At almost forty years of age, I was becoming adept in the art of the mosey. Meander, saunter, stroll, whatever you want to call it, I was quickly becoming a convert. Years of rushing to school, to work, to meetings faded into the background.

There was no need to rush, no need to hurry. Other than an occasional appointment or scheduled phone call with my investment advisor back East, I could be in the moment, remembering to breathe and enjoy the day. Although I passed no roses along my path, trust me. If I had, I would've stopped to smell them.

Minutes later I arrived at Caffe-Nation, and was greeted warmly by Mo.

"You're early," she told me. I was more of a mid-afternoon regular.

"Coffee," I begged her. "My first cup."

"Yikes," Mo said. "I've never seen you before your coffee."

"Robbie used to bring me coffee in bed," I confided. It felt kind of funny to say his name out loud. I had to say, I rather liked the feeling.

"Well, I'm bringing you coffee over here," she told me, as she brought a steaming mug to the table that I had just occupied.

"Bless you," I told her and breathing in the steam and heady aroma, proceeded to burn my tongue with the premature swallow.

"It's hot," I told her.

"I know," she said. "Customers get kind of pissy when it's not. Hey, that's the first time you've mentioned his name, at least to me," she added.

"Who, Robbie?" I asked her, a bit puzzled.

"No, Brad Pitt," she teased. "You really need that coffee, kiddo."

"Really, I mean, I talk about him a lot, at least it feels like I do."

"No, not so much," Mo responded. "But he sounds like a real catch. Breakfast in bed? Why did you let him get away?" she asked.

"I have no idea," I told her in all seriousness, "I honestly don't know."

"Sounds like someone needs a muffin," she told me. She was much better at changing the subject than I was. "Let's see, we've got cranberry orange, reduced-fat blueberry, lemon poppy seed."

"Too fruity," I protested.

"But wait, there's more," she assured me. And there were. After Mo hustled away to wait on other customers, I focused on the muffin I had chosen: a particularly luscious looking (and tasting) German chocolate number with coconut and pecan topping. Yum, cake for breakfast. That's a favorite of mine. The word luscious I mean. Sorry, that's me before coffee. I do enjoy cake for breakfast as well. Vowing to make one of my crowd-pleasing coffee cakes to share with Coop and Mo and Rick, too, I happily slurped coffee and proceeded to devour my muffin. Wiping away any telltale crumbs, I got rid of the evidence and went up to the counter for a refill but reluctantly passed on a second muffin. I found a local newspaper that another patron had abandoned, and spent a relaxing half hour catching up on all the world, regional, and local news that was fit to print. After leaving enough money to cover my breakfast as well as a generous tip (she was becoming a friend, but hey, she still deserved a tip) I headed back home.

Jagger was asleep on the patio near where I had originally spotted him. No sign of Coop. I slathered on SPF 50, donned a wide-brimmed hat and fell asleep on one of the recliners that Coop had so thoughtfully provided. I didn't wake up until my phone went off late in the day. It was Suze.

"What have you been doing?" she asked.

Not wanting to admit that I had slept in after a late-night having sex with my young, hot boyfriend, then went for coffee and a jumbo-sized muffin before settling in for a nap, I was noncommittal.

"Oh, you know, puttering, reading, cleaning the house." I didn't even believe me.

"Hmmm", Suze was suspicious. "It sounds like I woke you," she said accusingly.

I couldn't tell her. I mean, I'd hate me too. It's a tough life, but somebody had to live it. But in my defense, this was big for me. Huge, actually. I was changing, growing. Life in Sedona was so totally different than anything I had ever experienced. Not the Rick part. I mean, I've had passion in my life before. And certainly hotter sex. It's the "me" part. How I was learning to be in the moment, to go with the flow, to mosey. I knew that I would eventually find something meaningful to do with my life. But right then, I was just enjoying- time to read, to walk, to hang out with Jag. Change is good; I was learning to embrace it. To say that change has been something I've resisted in the past is a bit of an understatement. Let's look at the facts. I lived in the same house, my parents', for the first twenty-one years of my life. After they passed away, I moved to an apartment just a few miles away. It's a great town, okay? If it ain't broke, right? I enjoyed the college that I attended. Why not get my graduate degree there as well? I mean, I already knew where to park and the location of all the vending machines on campus. Hell, if it hadn't been for the lack of a PhD thing, I would have been happy to teach there. I'm like that with people, too. Long-term relationships are extremely impor-tant to me. I know first-hand just how fleeting life can be. I try to be a good friend and stay in touch with those I love.

Suze, Edie, Sarah, Kate? These women are my friends for life. I even get Christmas cards from old boyfriends. Well, one old boyfriend actually, and I'm pretty sure that the handwriting is his wife's, but you get what I mean, right? My bank and my cell phone provider hadn't changed in a decade. My chiropractor? Replacing Dr. Frank would be a challenge if and when the need arose.

But Robbie? Okay, it's complicated. Our divorce had thrown me for a loop. If I hadn't been so focused on my career, I would have been in really bad shape. That and the fact that we were talking every day or two and shagging every weekend. Yeah, that helped us to stay connected, alright. If I hadn't gotten divorced? Turned down for tenure? Lost my parents so early? Who knows where I might be? But those things did happen and I was here now. Ready for something wonderful to happen. I was content. Content and starving, I realized. On impulse, I called Coop. Did he want to grab a bite? Sure, why not? Sushi? Hell, yeah. I would convince him to stop for fro-yo on the way home. Maybe tonight, I would try something new, mix it up a bit? Who was I kidding? I would of course order the usual: salted caramel pretzel fat-free yogurt with chopped Kit-Kat bars. It was a classic and my current favorite. No need to change everything, right? But first things first, a shower and dinner for Jag. Some things never change.

CHAPTER 17

♫ You Can't Always Get What You Want ♫

never saw myself getting divorced. Hell, for that matter, I never saw myself even getting married. But I did get married and I did get divorced. Growing up, my parents' marriage was so rock solid that it was often difficult being a third wheel—two's company, three's just awkward at times. But I wasn't really alone. I had Claire. She was our house-keeper, chief cook, and bottle washer. Everybody should have a Claire. She wasn't a live-in. She went home to her husband every night, I guess to make his dinner and wash his dishes. She never spoke too much about her *other* life. I know she had lost a child several years before she came to us. What a stupid expression right? Lost a child like you might actually find it again like a pair of reading glasses or something. I overheard my parents talking about it one day. But in all the time I spent with Claire, the topic never came up. Claire worked for us from eight am to six pm Monday through Thursday. Fairly unusual arrangement, I guess, but it worked. She showed up mornings as my mom and I were heading out the door. She cleaned, did laundry, shopped for groceries, and prepared dinner for my family. When I got tired of hanging out at my folks' office after school, I often came home for cookies and conversation with Claire. I would tell her about my day and she would take a break from work, listen, and drink a huge mug of hot milky hot tea. Sometimes we would watch her favorite show, *General Hospital*. She'd get me started on my homework and often let me help her in the kitchen. So, you see I wasn't really alone, despite having parents 99% wrapped up in their work and each other. Mornings, I had my mom all to myself and afternoons, there was Claire. I think that's why I relate so well to other women and am so awkward around most men, except Robbie, that is. Once we got past the initial stages, I could be myself around Robbie. My true self. I loved him and trusted him completely. Still do.

But yes, cooking with Claire was a highlight for me. She was patient, made everything from scratch and was fearless when it came to substituting ingredients.

"Your dad doesn't care for onions," she would say, and toss in extra celery. "Your mom loves cilantro," she'd confide and set me to chopping up a pile. From Claire, I learned a lot about the positive impact a good meal can have on a frazzled family at the end of a crazy day. Also, how to perfectly roast a chicken, the special ingredient to add to a savory meatloaf (dijon mustard) and how to cook a tasty beef stew. My family loved her cooking and years later, Robbie did as well. I was never much of a homemaker, but the ability to whip up an occasional home-cooked meal was a good skill to have.

I did tend to be a homebody. I liked to go out, sure, but I really preferred to stay in. I was never much of a partier. I would nurse a glass of wine at a business function and sip beer with pizza when Robbie and I would go out with friends. But before you get the impression that I have no vices at all, hear this. My two pleasures in life? Coffee and ice cream, especially coffee ice cream—just about the best thing ever. Flowers may work for some girls, but show at my door with ice cream and I'm all yours. Really.

The first night in our new house, Robbie and I shared a pint of coffee mocha sitting on the floor of what would become our dining room once we had purchased a table and chairs. Oh, and lighting. As the old owners had taken all of the light bulbs out of the sockets, we moved around like thieves in the night. Also, no toilet paper, either. Stingy bastards. And we paid their asking price, too. We couldn't find candles—or even a spoon—in the dark among all those boxes, so we passed the melting ice cream back and forth, eating with our fingers and feeding each other. Things got messy and then things got sexy. When we woke up in the morning, we vowed to get completely unpacked and buy light bulbs for every lamp in every room in the house before it got dark. We did and eventually got things settled in our new place. It was probably five times larger than our old apartment, so we had fun buying furniture and accessories, pots and pans, and all kinds of housewares. We finally unpacked our wedding china and gifts and my folks' silver, none of which we used much over the years. We liked to entertain, but in a more casual way, usually centered around Robbie's grilled swordfish or salmon and my pasta salad. Okay, Claire's pasta salad. Formal meals just weren't our thing. We never really grew into the house. After almost six years, it remained too big for the two of us. We never needed that much space, and the months between Robbie's moving out and the sale of the place were the longest ever. I took to working even more, only coming home to make my way through the big, dark house to the guest room on the second floor. Robbie's ghost remained and I found myself in a very dark place for the first time since my parents' deaths fifteen years earlier.

I once again felt a strong sense of loss, but this time, it was mixed with feelings of failure. I blamed myself for the divorce. Not just because I wanted a career or anything. God, no. Maybe my standards were just too high, too unreasonable. I mean, if we didn't have the kind of all-consuming union of my parents, there must be something wrong, right? I guessed at what I thought normal was supposed to look like. I must have guessed wrong. If Robbie wanted to hang with his friends on a Sunday afternoon, that meant there was something wrong with us, right? It's not even that I wanted to spend all of our time together. I looked forward to an occasional night on the couch double dating with my old friends Ben and Jerry or going shopping and to lunch with a girlfriend on a Saturday. I just felt like we should be together or at least want to be together all the time and when we weren't, I assumed there was something wrong. I kept chipping away at that crack and the divide between us grew. We rarely fought, let alone argued, but we left a lot of things unsaid. Maybe we should have gotten out some of that anger we obviously both felt. Maybe yelled and screamed, then had great make-up sex. At least, I hear it's great. But I didn't know how to fight, not really, and Robbie must have been afraid to. Afraid that if we fought, then we would be the same as his parents had been. I probably should've felt a sense of relief when he left, since the last six months had been really horrible, but I didn't. At least, not at first. I felt sad and lonely and like I had screwed up my one chance at true love. I dated a few times over the next couple of years, but rarely more than once with anyone. I declined most setups and all blind dates. What is it about married people and their neurotic need to be with other married people or at least couples? Before I started spending my Saturdays with Robbie, I occasionally let a work colleague invite me to dinner, knowing that an eligible mutual acquaintance would be in attendance as well. Even Suze's husband got into the act, with a short string of bachelors. Maybe Suze encouraged him, as she clearly disapproved of my relationship with my ex.

"Give him a chance," she'd say, when I used a headache or an early morning as an excuse to leave early after one of her carefully arranged dinner parties. "Jax," she would plead as I grabbed my coat and proceeded to beat a hasty retreat. "Just stay for a while. He's really nice." I would hug her and tell her that it was okay. That I would make more of an effort next time. But I knew, deep down, it was very unlikely that I would meet the love of my life at my best friend's home. I had already met him. And he was gone.

Then I met Rick. For a while, I convinced myself that I was going to get a second chance at true love. But Rick wasn't it. I knew it almost immediately. Inconvenient, as I had taken a big chance and moved 2,500 miles to be closer to him. But Rick wasn't Mr. Right. Not really. But he was Mr. Right Now. And that would have to be enough. For now.

CHAPTER 18

♫ The Heart of the Matter ♫

"I never used to eat in places like this," Mo confided as we started to peruse the phonebook-size menus that our less than enthusiastic young waitress had left for us. I glanced around curiously. Places like this? A large sunny patio, splendid views of the red rocks, and a giant menu boasting that everything served was cage-free, antibiotic-free, hormone-free, and freakishly expensive. A Cobb salad for $27. Good Lord, did it come with a side of gold? I started to consider my dining options, when I suddenly smiled. I'd almost forgotten one of Robbie's most adorably annoying habits. He never opened a menu. Never. "What's good?" he would ask the server, placing his unread menu aside, as if he would take any and all recommendations to heart. Reactions were initially mixed, but within seconds, young waiters and older waitresses alike would be completely charmed, falling over themselves with their personal favorites and offers of options not even on the menu. "I'll have what he's having," I would occasionally wisecrack. Never even got a smile.

"Okay, I'll be right back with that," they would coo. Some of the females could carry it off, but if you've never seen a grown man coo, I do not recommend it.

"What? "Robbie the innocent would question when I glared at him. "People like to be helpful. It's in their nature. You just got to give them a chance, Jax." A chance indeed. I was a real 'Sally' when it came to ordering food in restaurants. You know the type. Coffee, black but only if it's just been brewed. Bread lightly toasted, dressing on the side, hold the onions. I can't help it. I want things how I want them. Wait staff hate me, I know they do. I can feel it is as they grip their pencil tightly, grind their teeth, roll their eyes, and struggle to maintain some level of civility as I patiently enumerate the substitutions, omissions, and cooking instructions that I am seeking. On the plus side, I'm an extravagant tipper. Really. I have been known to go as high as 50%. It drives me crazy when I see fellow patrons arguing over the check.

"You had a second glass of wine," or "my entrée cost less." Honestly people, you like each other enough to share a meal. Who cares who had what? Split the bill evenly and tell the wait staff to keep the change. If you can't afford to eat out, stay home. Learn to cook.

Mo and I had arranged to meet here for dinner on the one midweek evening that she had off at Caffe-Nation. I looked at her curiously.

"Places that actually serve food," she mused as she turned the pages between the pasta offerings and the vegetarian specials. *Say what?* I put my menu down and did that steeple thing with my hands and waited. It was the universal symbol for 'tell me more, I'm listening.' I didn't have to wait long.

"I'm a drunk, Jackie. A fall down, drink your whole paycheck kind of drunk." I gazed my new friend in amazement.

"What do you mean? I asked. "I've never seen you …"

"And most people I knew never have either. I hid it really well as long as I could. But that's all behind me now. I'm in recovery. Sober for two and a half years," she added proudly. "Good for you," I chirped. "Hey, drinking isn't all it's cracked up to be." Mo smiled at me.

"Yeah," she said sadly "it is." Despite the late afternoon sunshine spilling over the patio, I shivered. I had not seen that coming. We placed our orders with the less-than-perky Chelsea. The Southwestern chicken salad for me, grilled not fried, no onions, extra black beans, light on the cheddar, and extra dressing on the side. Chelsea was a trooper, I decided. What she lacked in charm, she made up for in dogged determination. She seemed hell bent on delivering on all my requests. Margarita pasta was Mo's simple order.

"Hold the tequila," she added.

"Oh, there's not really any tequila," Chelsea assured her.

"I know," Mo cut her off. "It's fine." Chelsea flounced away. I took a sip of my water. I was unsure how to broach the subject or even if I should. I took a deep breath.

"What happened?" I asked.

Her story was a simple one. Girl meets bottle. Girl falls in love with bottle. Bottle sets out to destroy girl. The blackouts didn't start until after her girlfriend Laura had moved out when they broke up after being together for four years. That was five years ago. After being promoted from assistant and taking the reins as principal at a large urban high school, the pressures started to mount. Teacher apathy, high dropout rates, and low test scores were the order of the day. Metal detectors were installed after a particularly nasty confrontation between rival gangs in the cafeteria. Attendance at monthly school board meetings became mandatory. Weekday hangovers and lost weekends had been the norm for most of her adult life, but the combination of loneliness and pressures on the job were growing. A couple of stiff drinks before the televised evening meetings became a habit.

"I couldn't show up unless I was a little high," Mo confided. "Those meetings were the worst. I didn't realize how much I drank that last night. Budgets were being cut and I was trying to justify saving the music program for my school. Listening to some clueless idiot from the Board of Education droning on about the benefits of shelving the music program and I just lost it. I grabbed the microphone and called him a fucking jerk. I dropped the F-bomb live on TV."

"Oh my God, you didn't."

"Yeah," she admitted. "I did. After that it was pretty straightforward. The school board asked for my resignation and I was out. Now I could drink whenever I wanted. No need to hide in the closet. Either closet." she grinned. "No need to keep up appearances. I ordered out and stayed in. The bank finally foreclosed and took my house. My brother pulled some strings and got me into treatment. For the first time in years, I was able to think. Think about my life and what I wanted.

"Then, I met a guy in recovery. He was young, in his early twenties, but he had traveled a lot. He kept talking about Sedona. He had been here on vacation with his family. It really stuck with him. "Sedona," he would say. "That's where I'm heading as soon as I get out of here."

"Is he here?" I asked.

"No," Mo was slow to reply. For the first time all night, she wouldn't make eye contact with me. *Uh oh.*

"Six weeks after getting released, he wrapped his car around a telephone pole back East. Ten in the morning and still high from the night before."

"Oh, that's terrible." I almost cried. Mo wasn't touchy-feely, but I reached over and grasped her hands in mine.

"It could've been worse," she told me. "He didn't hurt anyone else. *That* would've been terrible."

"And you?" I asked.

"I'm pretty good," Mo grinned. "Caffeine's my drug of choice these days. And sweets. So do you want to split something chocolate after this?" she asked mischievously as she dug into her pasta.

"Sure," I promised her, tucking into my salad. Crap, the chicken was fried. And that was definitely an onion slice. Damn you, Chelsea. I had such high hopes. Let it go, I told myself. Sedona-Jax would learn to deal. The rest of the evening passed quickly. Over coffee and a huge slice of vegan chocolate mousse pie, which tasted much better than it sounded, I told Mo all that had led up to my coming to Sedona. She knew bits and pieces from our conversations in the coffee shop. I confided just how painful it had been when I was denied tenure. Even though I had come up with a pretty fantastic contingency plan, it still hurt.

"I never did anything wrong," I told her. "The students loved me. My evaluations were off the charts. Must have been that one time I failed to start a new pot after taking the last of the coffee," I joked. I do that a lot. Deflect pain with humor. And chocolate. And I'd never really talked to her about Robbie. How we got together, how we broke up, and how he was still such a huge part of my life. I tried to gloss over the impact that Rick had played on my decision to move here. She had met him a few times when she waited on us, but I guess she must've assumed that I met him *after* I had moved here.

"So wait a minute. Are you telling me you quit your life back east and moved out here for *him*?" Stung by the judgment, I heard in her voice, I hurled back something along the lines of how at least I had a life to quit. *Ouch.* Awkward silence followed. I sipped the dregs of my coffee and racked my brain for what to say next. Mo beat me to it.

"Jackie, I'm sorry. I didn't mean to be critical. I have no right to judge you. I'm just so surprised. Rick seems so, so ..."

"So *what*?" I asked. "Do you think he's too young, too good looking for me?" Now it was Mo's turn to reach across the table and grasp my hands.

"God, no!" she said. "Of course not. That's not what I meant at all. It's just, I don't know. I think you deserve someone more substantial. I don't know, I mean he seems nice and all. Just, just not right for you."

"I know," I agreed. "He's not right for me. We're just friends. We hang out, and we talk, and sometimes we end up in bed, but that's all it will never be. No more than that."

"Are you okay with that?" Mo pressed.

"Yeah, I'm okay. He's not even that good," I confessed. Mo laughed heartily.

"Don't even get me started," she said. We split the check 50-50, after adding a sizable tip for Chelsea. We walked out back to the parking lot and realized that we had parked next to each other. Neither of us seemed to be in a hurry to rush off.

"So, what's the story with your ex?" Mo asked. "Do you still love him?" I looked at her.

"Yes, I do. I really do."

"Does he love you?" she asked.

"Yeah, he does." I know it. "He does," I admitted. Mo shook her head.

"What is it about you straight folks? You've got it so easy and yet you make it so hard."

"That's what he said," I laughed and hugged her. "Thank you. This whole evening has been so great. Let's do it again soon, okay?"

"Good night, Jackie. This *has* been great. See you tomorrow?"

"Sure" I told her. "I'll be the nonfat sugar-free vanilla latte, hold the whipped cream."

I drove home through the dark yet increasingly familiar streets of my neighborhood. I loved Robbie. I was still in love with my ex. There, I had said it out loud and I had a witness. Mo had heard me. Rick was wrong and Robbie was right? There it was. So, what was I going to do about it?

After I parked my car, I crossed the patio and could already hear Jagger meowing loudly. Despite the addition of Coop's recently installed cat door, my roomie usually waited for me before heading out at night. I let myself in and before I could even turn on the light, I scooped my furry friend up in my arms. Clearly not interested in cuddling, he struggled to be put down and raced out into the night. I figured maybe he needed some me-time. I had been out all night and now it was his turn. But I knew he'd be back in the predawn hours, seeking out my company and confirming that I was his human.

I changed into comfy sweats and plopped down on the sofa with my laptop and my phone. It was late, past midnight on the East Coast, but Robbie was a night owl. I sent him a text. 'R u up?' I held the phone tightly and willed him to respond. I really needed to hear from him. Just to let me know that he was still there, still Robbie. But my phone stayed silent. Either he was sleeping, or too preoccupied to answer my text. Had he found someone new? Someone pretty? Young? Less complicated? In the same zip code?

Lost in my thoughts, I sat there silently, growing increasingly glum and then I heard it. A light scratching on the door that told me Jagger was back. I tried to play it cool and looked away as he strolled in. I didn't want to appear needy. He strutted across the room and stood by his empty dish.

"So that's what you want," I accused him. "You came back for the food, not me." But he circled my ankles as I poured dry food for him and not much later, after I settled in bed with a book, he hopped up and made himself comfortable down by my feet, one paw resting on my ankle, and immediately fell asleep. Typical guy. I smiled. Just like Robbie. The man could fall asleep anywhere and so quickly. Back when we were still together, he would be asleep just a minute or two after his head hit the pillow. I would toss and turn and silently curse my peaceful, über-relaxed husband.

"What's your secret?" I would wonder. But that was Robbie. Made everything look easy. I loved that about him. I wished it had stayed easier with us. So where was my easy ex tonight? And who was he with?

CHAPTER 19

♫ I am Barely Breathing ♫

"First world problems," I interjected.

"What?" Suze asked with more than a hint of agitation.

"First world problems, Suze. You know, it's when ..."

"I know what first world problems are Jackie. Screw you."

Huh? "I mean it, go to hell."

"What is your problem, Susan?" I shrieked.

"It's always you, always about you. You are so dismissive of my problems, but God forbid, you get a hangnail." Suze's voice dripped with sarcasm.

"I don't know what you're talking about," I replied frostily. "I listen. I'm a good listener." And I rarely get hangnails.

"Yeah," Suze agreed. "You listen, then you jump in and make it sound like nothing. Or you turn it around and make it all about you."

I was stunned. Could that be true? Was I that self-involved to not care about someone else's problems, no matter how trivial they might be? Suze and I were having one of our regularly scheduled phone calls. She was on her lunch hour and I was still enjoying my third coffee on the patio. I had already tidied up and made the coffee, but that was about it. I have to say, living in a relatively small space all on one level is so practical. Efficient. Cleanup is a breeze, compared to the house I grew up in. Not that I spent any time doing household chores there either.

"You're so spoiled," Sarah and Suze would tell me repeatedly while we were growing up. I was always free to go out, hang out, or just chill. One or both of them was always stuck cleaning their room, babysitting younger siblings, or loading and unloading the dishwasher. I had no real responsibilities other than getting good grades and staying out of trouble. Neither of these expectations was actually communicated directly to me, but I had a strong sense that my parents preferred me at my high-performing, low-maintenance best. And I delivered. In spades.

But domestic chores really seemed to multiply when Robbie and I bought the big house early in our marriage. Suddenly weekends previously spent in bed or going to the movies or the mall were spent mowing lawns and scrubbing toilets. *Ugh.* Early on, we hired a crew to take over lawn maintenance as well as leaf and snow removal. We were both too busy and neither of us was particularly domesticated. The tools and equipment needed to complete these jobs were pricey and confusing and downright dangerous. Better to leave it to the professionals, we reasoned. I found a woman to come in to clean once a week. It was so nice to come home on Fridays to a house smelling of lemon furniture polish and slipping into a bed made up with clean sheets. We were a career couple after all, and the time we saved was better spent on our jobs or our relationship. Other than grocery shopping and schlepping the dry cleaning, I was free to focus on work and Robbie.

Since my move to Sedona, I was free to focus on um, well Jagger. No work, no Robbie. Mid-morning, you could usually find me in the middle of a strenuous walk/hike on a route that I had mapped out weeks ago. It was 3.2 miles of alternating high terrain and natural beauty. I would use the time to focus on my breathing and free my brain of all the thoughts and feelings usually whirling around. For a few precious moments, I tried to be all kinds of zen, and ignore the doubts, fears, and concerns, both major and minor, that usually dominated my waking hours. Should I get a job? What was going on with Rick? Should I keep Jagger in at night? Was Robbie dating? Where did I need to go to register to vote? What about global warming? And what's up with the economy? It's not easy being me sometimes. Honestly? It's friggin' exhausting.

After my daily walk, it was time for a shower and some lunch. I ate most of my meals on the patio, since it afforded the best views and overall ambiance. Sometimes I would read while I ate, other times listen to music or just visit with Jagger. He usually stayed close. How better to gobble up the bits of turkey or tuna that frequently made their way to him? Afternoons were spent running errands, hitting the grocery store, or visiting one of the boutiques that I had started to frequent. There was always something I needed for the house or a gift to send to someone back east. I had met a number of the various proprietors and artisans popu-lating the Uptown area and I grew to love the time to chat and window shop and make small purchases. I routinely stopped in for a mid-afternoon coffee and a visit with Mo at Caffe-Nation. Sometimes Rick would join me there if he got a break, and if there was a lull, Mo would sit with us and we would jabber on about all sorts of things. Local politics, world affairs, pop culture. I loved those times the best. Turned out Mo and Rick had very little in common besides me and both preferring women that is. Mo was extremely liberal and disagreed vehemently with all of Rick's right-wing conservative views on everything from gun control to welfare reform. I remained neutral, thanks to my easygoing demeanor combined with the fact that I am usually not well-informed enough to have much of an opinion on just about anything. So, I was usually silent when the discussions got heated, but I marveled at their ability to agree to disagree and remain cordial, even respectful of each other. I usually avoided conflict like the plague. But maybe arguments were okay, even necessary in a healthy relationship? *Hmmm …*

By late afternoon most days, I was back on the patio, catching up with emails and social media updates. I kept in touch with Sarah and Kate from back home and heard often from Edie, Robbie's step-mother. His mother and father had stopped talking to me since I had divorced their son, but honestly, I had never been that close with either of them and hardly noticed when the communication stopped completely. Once a week or so, I would have a beer with Coop over at the main house and I often met Mo in town for dinner on her night off. Rick and I would do dinner probably twice a week. Sometimes we went out, other times one of us, usually me, would cook. I enjoyed making a nice dinner for him and he seemed to appreciate my efforts. I will admit that it was good to have someone to cook for every once in a while. Left to my own devices, meal prep was non-existent. Sandwiches, cereal, eggs, yogurt with fruit. Those were my mainstays. The vegetarian thing was a bit tricky, but I was learning to make meatless substitutions to Claire's lasagna and chili recipes. Grilled portabella burgers were a big hit, too.

I still enjoyed Rick's company a lot. He was pretty witty in his way and always had lots of funny stories about his co-workers and the tourists he met. We kept it light and very casual. No long -term plans, and that was okay with me. I was living in the moment.

When Mo and I dined out, I would make up for all that healthy food with a steak or juicy cheeseburger. Guilt-free of course. And we always split some amazing dessert. Most nights that Rick and I got together, we also slept together. We had fallen into a routine early on. When he stayed with me, he would usually be up by six am to drive home and change for his early morning tour. When we started the night at his house, I usually drove home in the wee hours. I attributed my hasty exits to my cat's nocturnal habits, but honestly? I preferred my own bed and I liked waking up in my little home. Alone. I enjoyed the solitude and the privacy and the opportunity to snuggle with my main squeeze, Jagger. Not a lot of passion and zero drama. Rick and I were like an old married couple without the bills and the kids and the in-laws. Fine with me, I guess. It was all I needed for now.

I had planned to share some news with Suze that morning, but her snotty attitude changed my mind. I told her that I was sorry that she felt that our relationship was so one-sided and I promised to try harder. But honestly? The issues Suze had with her boss had been going on forever. It was hard to work up much in the way of righteous indignation at his chauvinistic behavior after all this time. Maybe I should practice heated responses like, "The nerve of that guy" or "Who does he think he is?" or maybe more sympathy like "Poor you." I knew that she got very little in the way of emotional support from her husband. He probably would prefer that she stay home and keep his house clean. But Suze was the main breadwinner, so that was not a real option. I vowed to do better, but once I hung up with her, it was back to being all about me. And how I could start giving back all that I had been given? So, not really about me.

I had been thinking about my future and how I could create something new. I'm not nearly as self-absorbed as I frequently appear, you see. I had been envisioning a new venture, a real opportunity. For weeks now, I had been tossing around an idea, something I could do with my life. I had never planned to take a permanent vacation. I knew I had a second act in me. I would run it by Mo and Rick that afternoon, maybe try it out on Coop as well.

I had been thinking about this for a while, the idea that all of us should get a second chance, an opportunity to rewrite the script for the second half of our lives. Maybe it was the knowledge that my next birthday would be my fortieth or all that had happened over the last year or two. I took a chance at a new life for myself, but I honestly hadn't risked that much, having a comfortable bank balance as a cushion. But there was a real need out there, I could see it. Mo told me frequently how exasperated she was, trying to find part-time helpers with both customer service skills and the computer savvy to work the café's relatively sophisticated ordering system and inventory program. Just in the short time I had been in Sedona, some of my favorite boutiques had already closed or gone under, due in part I imagined, to the owner's lack of business skills. Pricing and marketing strategies were flawed, and most small businesses appeared to be run by the seat of the over-burdened owner's pants. Even Rick, who rarely had a negative thing to say about anyone, bemoaned the work habits and skill sets of his younger co-workers. He recently sat in on an interview for a new driver, who had pulled out her phone and started texting.

"During the interview. Do you believe it?" he asked me incredulously. Yeah, sadly, I could. I had been in the classroom with these kids for many years. Their cell phones were their lifelines. So, I knew there was a real gap between the needs of local businesses and the current workforce. Since I had moved to Sedona, I had been meeting folks who were exploring the second phase of their lives: A computer tech turned tour guide, a school administrator turned barista, a high-level executive turned, well, Coop was still evolving. Maybe he could be my first client. There were others. Every shopkeeper, every artist, every waiter, or waitress had a past. They all had come here and morphed into something new. Reinvented themselves, or were trying to. The skills and resources needed to succeed varied, but maybe I could provide a centralized location, a one-stop shop if you will, in the form of a brick and mortar facility combined with a user-friendly website. Using social media to develop a network of opportunities, and a roster of locals to provide training: soft skills, computers, entrepreneurship, and marketing, I could help give folks of all ages and backgrounds inspiration and options to remake their lives. Turn their dreams into reality. I mean, what artist dreams about figuring out break-even price points? What fledgling jewelry designer finds true fulfillment setting up a business ledger? My business could provide low-cost counseling, workshops, and seminars, practical advice, and easy access to all of the resources needed to help the next Georgia O'Keefe among us to turn a profit. At least initially, I would focus on two main audiences: business owners looking to grow their businesses and hourly workers looking to obtain more fulfilling careers.

Over the next few days, I ran my ideas and preliminary plans by everyone I knew.

"Sounds like a consignment shop," Mo offered when I tried out names for my new venture: "Second Chance," "Take Two," and "2nd Act" were rejected by Edie as well. Rick was somewhat intrigued and offered to scout out properties for me. A physical storefront in a prime location would be expensive, but necessary in order to get potential clients and employers talking. Nothing got Sedona-ites buzzing like a big grand opening, according to Rick. Robbie was supportive and more excited than just about anyone. With his characteristic insight and creativity, he helped me to create a detailed business plan during our regular phone calls. He asked good questions, tough ones, and got me thinking about just what programs and services my new venture could offer. But my new venture still lacked a name.

One night, it hit me. I was sitting on the couch reading. Jagger had stayed in for the night and was curled up next to me, one paw possessively claiming my left ankle. I dialed Robbie's number, knowing full well that it was ridiculously late even for a night owl like my ex. He answered on the third ring.

"Jax, what's up? You okay?" *Hmmm.* He sounded like he was awake. Wide awake. It was one a.m. on the East Coast. What had he been up to? Why was it any of my business? Was someone there with him? I pushed these negative thoughts out of my mind.

"I'm great, Rob. ENCORE. ENCORE, what do you think?"

"It's terrific. Easy to remember, great for branding. Yeah, that's it," was his immediate reply. I gotta give the guy credit.

It had been a couple of days since we spoke, and while the new business venture was always on my mind, I couldn't really expect that it would be top of mind for anyone else. But that was Robbie. There were no flies on him. He got it, got me. As a woman from Australia whom I met years ago at a conference would have said, 'I landed in the tall grass with that one.' How had I managed to screw things up so royally? We chatted for a few more minutes and after offering to create some logo concepts, he told me how proud he was of me, and how glad he was that I was pursuing this new and exciting opportunity. A lump formed in my throat and threatened to turn into tears: of gratitude, of nostalgia, and of despair. I missed him, damn it, I wanted to be in the same room with him at that moment. Sharing way more than just a late night call. I ended with a hasty "Thanks, love," and hung up. "This sucks, Jag," I howled. "What am I doing?" Maybe I deserved a second chance as well. Not just at work, but in my life. Next time the subject of Robbie coming to visit came up, I would follow up. Offer to check flights or suggest a specific timeframe. I would let the details work themselves out later. Like where he would sleep and if I should let him meet Rick. Just jump in. Yeah, that's it. I hopped up and off the couch so suddenly that I disturbed Jag's grooming efforts. Ignoring his disdainful glare, I picked him up and swung him around.

"You're going to meet him," I promised Jagger. "Robbie is coming to visit us." Underwhelmed by the news, Jagger struggled to be put down, and seconds later disappeared through his cat door. "You'll see. You'll love him," I promised his retreating form. *Just like I do.*

CHAPTER 20

♫ Key West Intermezzo ♫

"Jax?"

"Yeah, Suze?"

"I hope you still feel small when you stand beside the ocean."

"Huh?"

"I hope you still feel ..."

"Yeah, I heard you. What're you talking about?" That second margarita at lunch had done her in. I stopped at one, but Suze was still feeling the effects of all that tequila combined with the scorching hot sun. And she had been throwing back wine coolers since we got back to the hotel. She was shit-faced.

"It's just that, I don't know Jax. I just have this feeling." I let the folded t-shirt that had been protecting my face from the sun fall as I struggled to sit up straight.

"Suze? What is it? What's wrong?"

"I don't know exactly." My best and oldest friend was struggling. It was not just the alcohol talking. "I just miss you, I guess, and I love you. This trip is just, I don't know, the best. You know how grateful I am, right?"

It was late in the afternoon of another glorious Key West day, and Suze I were lounging on the balcony of our deluxe hotel room with an indescribable view of the water. It was the fourth day of a vacation planned hastily the week before. I woke up one day in my new Sedona home and I swear I had been dreaming about the ocean. Crashing waves, seagulls, golden sand, the whole deal. I'm not much of a dreamer or if I am, I barely remember my dreams. But as I lay there that morning in the moments before I was fully awake, the dream seemed so real that I could smell the salt air and feel the warm sun. Reality in the form of a full bladder and a hungry Jagger took over and it was later that morning before the memory washed over me once again. I knew one thing. I had to get to the ocean and soon. I was suddenly painfully aware of the physical shortcomings of my landlocked new home. Growing up on the East Coast, I guess I must've taken the ocean for granted. I mean it was always there, a relatively short drive to the Cape or the Connecticut shoreline and only a bit longer to get to the coast of Maine. But the reality of living in the land of desert and rocks hit me that morning. I suddenly felt restless and knew what I needed to do.

First, I called Suze and talked her into meeting me in Florida later that week. Maybe she was missing me or maybe she just needed some time in the sun, but she wasn't hard to convince. I raced next door and got Coop to agree to watch Jagger for me. A few minutes online and I had secured airfare for both Suze and myself. Our flights would arrive within an hour of each other in Miami and a rental car would get us to Key West in just a few hours. Based on location and a five-star rating, I reserved a deluxe room for the two of us for five nights. It is amazing how fast you can pull things together if you really put your mind to it. I chose Key West for purely sentimental reasons. From a trip that Robbie and I had taken seven or eight years ago, I remembered the lively bustle of Duval Street and the gorgeous sunsets from Mallory Square. Endless beaches. Lively nightlife. Good shopping. I couldn't remember the name of the hotel where we stayed back then, but it didn't matter. Not really. Suze and I would make some new memories there and get to spend some quality BFF time together. I emailed the details of our upcoming itinerary to Suze and printed a copy for Coop. After all that excitement and feeling very satisfied with my progress, I decided to stroll into town for an iced something or other at Caffe-Nation.

"What's it been?" Mo asked when I told her about my upcoming trip. "A few months?" I thought back.

"You mean since I moved here? Yeah, about that. Why?"

"Yeah," she said, nodding vigorously. "That's when it really hits you."

"What?"

"The reality. Sedona. Oh, it's beautiful and lovely and all that, but it's not for everyone."

"I'm not getting you," I said. "What's not for everyone?"

"The isolation, the desert. It draws people in, but after the novelty wears off, it's just too much or maybe it's not enough for some people."

"What are you saying?" I asked. "That I don't belong here?" *God, I was needy.* She paused, before answering thoughtfully.

"No, you belong here, probably more than most. You just need a dose of reality, or your past, or maybe you just miss your friend. What do I know? I make lattes for a living?"

I talked to Rick that night. He called me right after finishing his last tour, wanting to get together. After only a short time as an unofficial couple, the bloom was already off the rose. The honeymoon period had ended. We still talked every couple of days, but we only got together once or twice a week and rarely spent the whole night together. Meeting for dinner was good or an occasional hike, frequently followed by some fairly energetic, if uninspired sex, but I wasn't looking for more, and he seemed fine with me as a pal and occasional bedfellow. I loved how uncomplicated he was, but I had been jonesing for more intimacy, more passion, both in and out of the bedroom. But it wasn't going to happen. Not between us. I asked for a rain check and said I would call him the next day. But before I hung up, I told him about my upcoming trip and my conversation with Mo.

"Yeah," he agreed. "She's right. A few months seems to be about the point that a lot of people realize exactly where they are and where they're not. Coop calls it a stop-pause. It's like going stir-crazy. Sedona's great, but it's not for everyone." *Sedona's great, but it's not for everyone.* Call the Chamber of Commerce, folks. It's the tourist-repelling catch phrase we've been waiting for. I hung up feeling vaguely unsettled. Was Sedona right for me?

So a few days later and here we were. We slept late every morning and enjoyed brunch at a number of elegant eateries that seemed to dominate Key West. We usually spent afternoons walking the beach and frolicking in the surf. I know, what a picture, right? A couple of middle-aged women dashing in and out of the waves and searching for the perfect seashell or piece of sea glass. After a late afternoon nap in the shade, we would take our showers, get all dolled up, and join the masses on Duval Street. Shopping in the touristy gift shops that populated Key West, I bought t-shirts for Rick and Coop. Rick's was easy, light grey XL with a simple message. '*I got Duval faced on Shit Street.*'

Coop's took more time. I debated the merits of a humorous message versus a more classic design. And the size? M or L? What was he? Finally Suze snapped at me.

"Oh God, it's just a t-shirt. Buy that one in medium and that in large and decide which to keep and which one to give Cooper later."

"It's Coop," I corrected her. "And what's gotten into you?"

"I don't know, sorry. Take your time, I'm fine. Whatever. Don't worry about me." *Hmmm. A crabby Suze? That was a new one. Opinionated, outspoken, and judgmental? Sure, but rarely crabby.* I decided quickly on the shirt with a classic Key West logo in a Large. They shrink anyway, I reasoned. In a lovely nearby jewelry store, I found a silver and turquoise bracelet for Mo. I tried to find something new for Jagger, but what do you get the cat that has everything? Including me, apparently. Wrapped around his little paw. Earlier that morning, Coop had texted me a photo of my little fellow sleeping in the sunshine on the patio and I almost cried.

"Suze, does he look sad to you? Do you think he misses me?" Never an animal lover, Suze concurred.

"I'm sure he misses you, Jax. I'm sure he can't wait to see you again," she reassured me over margaritas and fish tacos.

"Yeah," I said slightly mollified. "I bet he does."

"So what's next?" she asked.

"What, tonight? I don't know. Go for a walk, maybe rent a movie? What sounds good?" I was relaxed and had no agenda. No list.

"No, I mean what's next for you?" Oh, okay. I wasn't stupid. I knew she was looking for me to clarify my situation. Rick? Robbie? Or what? Despite non-stop talking since the moment when we hugged at the airport, we hadn't had *the* talk.

"Oh Suze, I don't know. I mean what's the rush? I'm happy. Be happy for me. I don't know what will happen. Does anyone? I just, I don't know."

"You said it's not serious with Rick. You don't have a job. I mean, maybe you should just come home."

Home? Was that it? I wondered. Did Suze just miss me? Or did she think that I had made a mistake in moving? Or worse, maybe she thought I was regretting the decision, once it had become crystal clear that Rick and I were not 'Rick and I?' But what about ENCORE? I would have a business to run if I ever got it off the ground. I shrugged noncommittally. Going back to Massachusetts was not an option, but I didn't feel like arguing or defending my steadfast position on the subject. Sensing that it was not one that was up for further discussion, Suze launched into the pros and cons of purchasing a pricey pair of earrings she had spotted earlier that day. I was grateful for the change of topic and listening to her jabber on, I realized just how much I missed her. I reached for her hand, across the table, which was crowded with empty glasses and our dinner plates that had just about been scraped clean. When I say those were good fish tacos, believe me. Really good.

"I love you, you know?" I told my oldest friend. She grasped my hand in hers.

"Love you more." So, we were good, for now at least.

The next day, I got bit by the spending bug. We visited a really upscale boutique where I found a gorgeous pet bed made of rattan with a striped pillow that incorporated the brilliant hues that I associated with Key West—brilliant coral, lime green, and deep aqua.

"It'll be like bringing some of the Keys with me back to Sedona," I babbled. I arranged for shipment, as it was far too bulky to ever consider taking with me. Her eyebrows raised as the store associate quoted the fee to ship Jagger's new throne, Suze was strangely silent as we left the store.

"What?" I asked her.

"Nothing, I'm fine," she responded quickly. Wandering down the street, the next store we came to featured classic Adirondack furniture in a rainbow of colors, including my aforementioned favorite three. I quickly purchased a chair in each color and two small side tables in a golden yellow. *What the hell?* I told myself. I was living in a partially-furnished guesthouse and I wanted to express myself with furniture for my patio. Sue me. Coop and Jag would love it. Suze remained fairly quiet during my spree and we returned to the hotel to lounge on the deck prior to showering before dinner. Soon after, Suze started on the wine coolers.

"So why am I supposed to still feel small?" I asked her. Suze rolled on her side to face me.

"You're amazing," she told me. "Even after your folks died and Robbie left and you didn't get tenure, you're the most positive person I know. I just don't want that to change. The money, I mean, it's great, but don't become *that* person. The one who doesn't look at price tags, collects expensive baubles, and doesn't understand how the rest of us live." Swallowing a defensive retort, I forced myself to remember. *This is Suze. She loves you. She means well. She's a little drunk. Was it about the money I had just squandered or was there something else going on?* She's just never seen this side of you before, I told myself. No one has.

"I won't. I promise. I just got a little carried away, Suze," I promised. "Jeez, one minute you're telling me to buy two t-shirts and the next you're complaining that I'm buying a few pieces of furniture. What do you want from me?" Suze gulped and looked miserable. I struggled on, trying to bring a smile to her dear, familiar if somewhat tipsy face.

"I promise. I'll never lose that sense of wonder. And I'll make sure that when one door closes, that one more opens. And I'll dance, okay? I will dance." Relieved that she hadn't been too over-the-top voicing her concern, and fully aware that I was mocking her, Suze swung around and flipped her towel in my direction as she headed toward the bathroom.

"Just for that, I may or may not leave you any hot water. Or a clean towel."

"That's ok, I'll buy more," I teased. I lay back on the chaise and watched the sun as it continued to set. The spending would stop as soon as I got back. I knew this. I would once again compare prices and reconsider my need for big purchases *Ad nauseum*. My frugal self would return, I had no doubt. Relaxing again, I realized that we would have to get a move on if we were going to join the crowd down on Mallory Square and claim sunset-watching chairs similar to the ones I had just purchased. But I didn't feel like rushing. I didn't feel the need to cross something off my 'to do' list. Maybe for tonight, I would let things just happen. As soon as I returned to reality, I would really need to buckle down. I had interviews scheduled, employees to hire and preliminary meetings set up with a few accounting firms. I planned to narrow down my choices of storefront properties that Rick identified for me and to start ordering office furniture and supplies. Oh, and pick up phones and a couple of computers. But there was nothing I could do about any of that right now. Tonight, I would just relax and enjoy this time with Suze, assuming that a long, hot shower sobered her up some. I closed my eyes for a moment, then I remembered. I hopped up and banged on the bathroom door. Over the pulsating rhythm of the shower, I reminded my best friend that we had made dinner reservations for that night. Another highly-recommended seafood restaurant. Any fresh catch of the day was fine as long as it was cooked to order; grilled, blackened, or steamed. I only had another couple of days with Suze in this tropical paradise. Tomorrow, we would definitely have to look into renting a Sunfish or a couple of kayaks or try paddle boarding. I vowed to surround myself with water as much as possible until we arrived back at the airport. I would be back in the land of cacti and red rocks soon enough.

CHAPTER 21

♫ Losing My Religion ♫

What was I going to do about Robbie? It had been nearly a week since he left Sedona and the only contact with me that he had initiated was a text telling me that his return flight had arrived home on time. Other than that, nothing. Nada. Total silence. I wasn't really surprised. I mean, things had gotten kind of weird at the end of his visit, at the beginning, too. But the middle? Oh, nothing weird about the middle. I'm blushing, okay? The guy can still make me blush. I am still crushin' on my ex, there is no doubt. After weeks of dancing around the inevitable, we had finally scheduled Rob's first trip to Sedona.

When I drove to Phoenix to pick him up at the airport, I felt giddy and excited. I wasn't sure what to expect, but I figured I would find out soon enough. When I saw him exit the terminal and walk towards my illegally parked car (it was the white zone and I was loitering, not loading or unloading, but c'mon, his flight was nearly a half hour late) my heart stopped. Honest, at the very least it skipped a beat. He came striding towards me, walking briskly, and grinning like a fool. Or maybe that was me. He saw me as I got out of my car and he hurried towards me.

"Jax, hey, I made it," he told me and swept me up into a massive bear hug. I told you, he has no qualms about showing his feelings in public, right? He broke off first and holding me by the shoulders, looked me over and grinned even more.

"God, you look great."

"You too," I assured him. And he did. We stowed his luggage in my trunk and took off towards Sedona. I chattered on and on and was trying to describe the types of cacti we would see during the drive. I was about to tell him how there are no saguaro cacti in Sedona and how he shouldn't purchase any souvenirs that made it look like there were. He cut me off, before I could finish.

"Oh, has the deluxe tour already begun?" *Ow, is my nose bleeding?* I'd just been tagged. An awkward silence followed. I concentrated on the road clogged with normal Friday afternoon traffic. Robbie finally broke the silence.

"Sorry, Jax. I didn't mean anything by it. I just, I don't know. I keep thinking about you and that guy, that tour guide." Okay, we were officially in awkward-ville, population two.

"It's okay, Rob. It'll be fine." I tried to reassure him. And it would be, too. I had it on good authority that my ex and my sorta boyfriend wouldn't be crossing paths, not this weekend at least, or ever, if I had anything to say about it. It was mid-January and Rick was staying at his buddy's house in Cottonwood for several days to remodel the bar area at his restaurant. He had teased me about the timing the last time we spoke. I was glad he couldn't see my face or the flush that had appeared when Rick mentioned Robbie's name.

"So I'm leaving for a few days and Rob comes to visit. How convenient." I figured he was kidding with me when he said it.

"It's not like that," I protested. "It's, it's ..."

"Complicated," Rick finished for me. "Yeah, I get it." Was he pissed, or jealous, or just trying to give me a hard time? I couldn't really tell. Even after six months of regularly keeping company, Rick remained an enigma to me. Our relationship had yet to be defined. Were we Facebook official? I doubted it. Rick didn't have a computer, let alone a profile, and my own updates since moving here were strictly photos and accompanying comments of the 'Jag napping' or 'Jag chillin' variety. Occasionally, I would post a photo of yet another gorgeous Sedona sunset, but I kept mum about anything remotely personal.

"So," I began tentatively, "we haven't really talked about what you want to do while you're here." And we hadn't. One hundred percent of our conversations about his visit concerned travel logistics, no discussion of how we would spend our time or where.

"I know you've always wanted to see the Grand Canyon, right?" At Robbie's nod of assent, I pushed on. "I don't know if this is the best time of year for that, though. Maybe if you come back this spring, it'll be better. But there's plenty to do here. We could go for a hike and hit Uptown." Silence.

"Damnit, Rob. Help me out here. I'm doing all of the work." Robbie laughed.

"It's good to see you, Jax. I forgot just how much you like to plan everything." Stung again, I retreated into silence once more and focused my attention on the road. *Screw you, Rob.* After several minutes (it just felt like more) Robbie started things up again.

"Rides nice."

"Huh?"

"The car, it rides nice. Are you happy with it?" I had purchased my new car just a couple of days prior to leaving last

June and as such, Robbie had never ridden in it.

"It's good, I like it. The gas mileage is pretty good, I guess, but then, most days I don't even drive it." See, normal conversation between normal people. We could handle this. "Did you want to stop along the way to eat? I'm sure they didn't feed you on the plane. Not trying to over plan, but after this next exit, there's not too much to pick from until we get to Sedona," I told him.

"I could eat," Robbie responded, "but I want to check out Sedona. Hit some of your favorite places. So, let's wait." Now that we had a basic plan, I could relax, but not too much, as the roads down here were not all that familiar to me and it was now totally dark. Robbie told me about his work and what he had been doing. Ironically, the overnight travel that was so common during the last few years of our marriage had petered out and Robbie was getting restless. His agency had lost a few key accounts and although none of them had been assigned to him, it cast a pall on the whole office and rumors of layoffs were becoming quite commonplace.

"Are you okay?" I asked him. "Are you worried?" The promise of a partnership had never materialized even after all that travel and his success as a rainmaker. I knew that Robbie had become increasingly disillusioned about his future at the agency, but I hadn't realized that it was this bad.

"I'll be fine, Jax, don't worry. You know me." At that, he reached over and squeezed my hand. "It's good to be here. I've missed you," he said simply.

"Ditto," I replied lightly and squeezed his hand back.

We ended up eating grilled salmon burritos in Uptown Sedona at Oaxaca, a place that had become a favorite of mine. Used to seeing me with Rick or Mo or even one time with Coop, the hostess greeted us warmly and offered us a choice of seats.

"Crystal will be right over to take your order, Jackie."

"Thanks, Joanne," I replied.

"Come here often?" Robbie asked and I nodded.

"It's so good. You'll love it," I told him.

"I'll have what she's having," Robbie said after I ordered and described exactly how my entrée should be prepared. Crystal laughed as if it was the funniest thing she had ever heard. Honestly, she was way too young to have gotten the *When Harry Met Sally* reference. Robbie's ability to charm everyone he came into contact with was alive and well. Robbie passed on a margarita and so did I. Lately I found myself drinking even less than I had back East, as my local best pal was in recovery and my boyfriend and my landlord both stuck with a couple of beers while out or more frequently, unsweetened iced tea. I drank a couple glasses of water while we waited for our food. The service that night was good and the food was, as always, amazing.

"I can't eat another bite," Robbie moaned, as Crystal swooped over to remove his plate.

"I know, right? The salmon combined with black beans and feta and chopped cucumber. So good, right?" Robbie agreed and asked for coffee, but I told him that dessert was waiting for us back at my place and that I could make coffee as well. When we left the restaurant a little later, Joanne winked at me and gave me the thumbs up sign. Oddly comforting, but weird.

Back out on the street, the wind had really kicked up and we race-walked to the car. We clambered in and before buckling up, ended up in an embrace that turned into a kiss. On the lips. Oh God, kissing Robbie- clearly one of the great pleasures in life. I hadn't forgotten exactly, but wow. I was in trouble. I pulled away first and told him that we should get going, that Jagger needed feeding.

"Oh, yeah, I get to meet the famous feline tonight," he remembered. "I sure hope he likes me," he teased.

Remembering how Jag had faked a fur ball the first time he met Rick, I noted drily, "he's kind of weird around strangers. Don't expect too much." I need not have warned him. When we first arrived home, Jagger made no bones about his displeasure with me on the lateness of his dinner and the fact that I had brought a stranger home as well. Before I could give Robbie the cook's tour, I hurried to get dinner ready for His Highness while he looked around.

"I love what you've done with place," he drawled. I looked up.

"No really, Jax, it's great. It's you," he assured me. Waiting for his dinner to be served, Jag's interest in our guest was minimal. While he dug into his evening meal, we looked out through the big window.

"The patio is where I spend most of my time, even in the winter. Those are the chairs I got in Key West. Remember I told you? Nice, huh?" Robbie's approval was important to me. He had exquisite taste, really spot on. At this point in the tour, we were approaching the bedroom. Hoping Robbie would not make any cracks about how that must be where the magic happened or something equally awkward, I just kind of pointed.

"So that's the bedroom. Where I sleep. It's really quite large."

"That's what she said," Robbie laughed. I joined him. That man could always make me laugh. Even when he could also make me cry.

"So, I'll start some coffee," I told him and walked ten feet to the safer, more neutral kitchen location. There had been no magic happening in the kitchen, culinary or otherwise.

"Decaf, okay? But only if you're having some," Robbie added.

"Sounds good," I told him. As I brewed a pot of decaf (the real thing- no blueberry, no hazelnut, just coffee sans caffeine) I got Rob busy unwrapping the box of desserts that Mo had provided for the occasion.

"She's great. You'll love her," I told Robbie.

"I already do," Robbie assured me as he surveyed the assortment. Raspberry squares, blonde brownies, red velvet cupcakes with cream cheese frosting, and tarts topped with lemon custard and blueberries.

"I don't eat like this every day," I told him.

"I can see that," he assured me. "You look great."

"You too, Rob." *Really great.*

We settled on the couch with our coffee and desserts, but before we had a chance to dig in, Jagger made his move. Strutting boldly and purring loudly, he leapt up on the couch and proceeded to properly greet our guest. Pushing his tawny head at Rob, he head-butted and rubbed himself against his new best friend.

"Well hey, big fella," Robbie greeted him and proceeded to scratch and pet every body part that Jag proudly presented. "Yeah, he's definitely not okay with strangers," Rob kidded me as, finally sated, Jag circled around and curled up on his lap. Lucky cat!

As we drank our coffee and nibbled on some of the amazing desserts, we caught each other up on all of the details of our new lives. Despite talking on the phone two or three times a week, and countless texts and emails, there was still so much to say to each other. When I caught my visitor from the East Coast stifling a yawn for the third time, I suggested that we call it a night. After Robbie decided that a shower could wait until the morning, he helped me make up the pullout couch that he would sleep on during his stay. As if by some unspoken agreement, it was clear that there would be no shenanigans of any sort that night. I fussed over the skimpy mattress, but he reassured me.

"It'll be fine, Jax. You know me, I can sleep anywhere." And he could. By the time I came out of the bathroom after checking out the mostly familiar toiletries that Robbie had unpacked, I tiptoed past a sleeping ex-husband and the happy feline curled up by his head.

"Kiss ass," I whispered and went into my bedroom to sleep alone. Maybe it was the long drive or the big meal or the secure feelings that Robbie always provided or all of the above, but I fell asleep quickly and slept soundly.

I woke to the unmistakable aroma of fresh-brewed coffee. *Luxury.* I started to get up to investigate, just as Robbie came in balancing a tray. His huge grin quickly turned to a look of concern when he saw my reaction.

"Oh Jax, don't cry. C'mon. It's okay." Tears streamed down my face as I struggled to not lose it.

"Oh Robbie," I sobbed. "Thank you. You don't know how much this means to me," I told him. In addition to the coffee, he had poured juice and sliced the coffee cake that I had baked yesterday. I felt like a queen.

"I missed this cake," he told me as we dug in.

"I missed you," I told him. I was halfway through my second cup when Robbie decided that he needed a shower. He hustled off, while I continued to sit in bed. Jagger sat in the doorway and watched me as I wiped away crumbs and stacked the tray. He looked annoyed. Annoyed at me. I swear he disapproved of my making his new favorite male human sleep on the couch.

"Don't judge me," I told him. "It's complicated." But suddenly it wasn't. Complicated. It was simple, plain to see and so very obvious. The man of my dreams, the love of my life, my soul mate, my best friend was naked and soaking wet and I was sitting in bed bone-dry and very much alone just a few feet away. What was wrong with this picture? Had Sedona-Jax lost her mind? I needed to sort out my priorities. Time to get with the program. I hopped up and crossed the room.

"Go get him," I told myself. Morning breath, bed head and all, I knocked on the bathroom door. Just once and let myself in. Robbie was happy to see me. Real happy. It was familiar and new and steamy and very hot and unlike a Sedona sunset, it was *not* over way too soon. Not by a long shot.

The next few days flew by. Robbie got to meet Coop and Mo and to explore Sedona. And me. Again and again. We took several long hike/walks and he was awed by the rugged beauty that surrounded my new home. He helped me to decide on the location for ENCORE and even glanced over the resumes I had been collecting for the two positions I was looking to fill. His enthusiasm for my new venture was contagious and lots of decisions that I had been dragging my heels on suddenly got made. Everything was great until the last evening. Rob had been uncharacteristically subdued all night. I was recounting what we could do the next day before we had to leave for the airport.

"You still haven't been to Oak Creek," I told him. "or Tlaquepaque Village. Maybe we can have breakfast at that place that Coop mentioned. Should we ask him to join us?"

Silence.

"Rob?" I asked. "What do you think?"

"No, Jax," he said, as he fiddled with his smartphone.

"No Coop, no breakfast? What?" I was confused. Was he pissed off? Why the silent treatment. Had I tired him out or was he just bored?

"No, I mean, you guys should go. I'm gonna take off early," he finally offered.

"No Rob, your flight's not 'til one," I corrected him. "We could ..."

"No, Jax, I'm going to fly from Sedona. I got a flight at eight a.m. I'll have plenty of time to connect in Phoenix." Yeah, about four hours, I realized.

"Why? I don't get it." I protested. I was about to reassure him that driving him to Phoenix was no problem when he stopped me.

"I've gotta go, Jax," he told me sadly. "It's time." Okay. I didn't argue.

We spent an hour on the couch with Jag happily ensconced between us. Robbie seemed to be intent on following some cop show that we used to watch. My thoughts were swirling and I was unable to focus. I had known that he was going to leave and that everything that had happened between us could not be ignored, but I didn't want to spoil our time together. I hoped that we would eventually talk and schedule a follow-up or figure something out, but I wanted to hold off for now and just enjoy our last night together. A short while later, we made the mutual decision to turn in and I was pleased when he joined me in bed. I had thought he might choose to occupy the couch like he had the first night.

"Good night, sweetheart," he told me and kissed my cheek. He fell asleep almost immediately, while I tossed and turned. Nothing's changed, I thought. We're great in bed. We're divorced. We've moved on. Haven't we? I slept fitfully and woke up feeling tired and anxious.

We had time for a quick coffee in the morning, standing at the breakfast bar. I had gotten up first and had everything ready when he came out of the bedroom wheeling his carryon. Would he have brought coffee to me in bed? Maybe. I'll never know. We made the short drive to the Sedona airport in awkward silence. He insisted that there was no need for me to come in to the tiny terminal, so after a quick kiss and a "Thanks for everything, Jax," he was gone. That was it. I cried all the way home and didn't leave my place, not even for a walk, for the next few days.

CHAPTER 22

♫ You're My Home ♫

"I love him so much," I gushed. "He's just the best. I have no idea what I did before he came along." Suze was not convinced.

"I don't know, Jax. I mean, I can see what he gets out of it. Food, company when he wants it, freedom when he doesn't." I started to protest when Suze cut me off. "You've already told me, he comes and goes as he pleases, right?"

"Well yeah, but you gotta understand. Before me, he was completely on his own. Being with me is a big step for him, you know?"

"Okay, maybe this is one of those times that we need to agree to disagree," Suze conceded. Whatever. After we hung up, I went to find him. Just as I suspected, he was laying on my bed with his back to the door.

"Oh don't be like that," I told him. "I can't be snuggling with you and catching up with Suze at the same time, ok?" I tried to lie down next to him to resume the half-nap/ half-cuddle session that Suze's call had interrupted. But Jag wasn't having it. Deftly, he jumped off the bed and left the room, his long tail standing straight up in silent protest. Seconds later, I heard the unmistakable sound of the cat door swinging shut as Jagger went off to do cat things without me.

Well, I had bigger fish to fry anyway. I still did not know what I was going to do about Robbie.

After that one text message, it was all quiet on the Eastern front. Not a word. I kept all other human contact to a minimum. No, not because I wanted to keep the lines open in case Robbie called, as I had call waiting. No, it was even simpler—I had nothing to say. Me—who was almost never at a loss for words. I was sad and broken and empty. Jag stayed close as if he could sense my pain. I talked briefly with Suze by phone and once with Coop, while standing in the doorway when he brought my mail over. I slept a lot and moved around my little home like a zombie. A very lonely one. I hadn't heard a single word from Rick for over a week, which wasn't at all unusual, since it was rare that we called each other just to chat. I assumed that he was still out of town or maybe he had returned and was waiting for me to tell him that the coast was clear. Whatever. I didn't really care one way or the other. I hunkered down and moped. Mo stopped by with a large latte and a banana chocolate chip muffin late one morning.

"Oh sweetie, you've got it bad, don't you?" she hugged me and watched me sip my drink and pick at my breakfast. I sniffed in agreement.

Mo glanced around and I'm sure that she noted the clutter resulting from stacks of unopened mail and empty take-out containers spilling over my normally neat countertops. They were a mess. So was my life.

"We need to get you outta here, Jax. What do ya say?" Mo asked.

"Hmmm. No, I'm fine. I don't know. Maybe," I offered.

"So how about dinner tomorrow night, huh? My treat. But it'll have to be an early night, okay? I've got a date. A hot date," she added mysteriously. When I failed to respond, she trilled,

"Ooh. A date. Who's the lucky girl, Mo?" Okay. I can play along.

"Who's the lucky girl, Mo?" I wondered aloud.

"Joanne", she admitted happily.

"Wait, Joanne, the hostess at Oaxaca, Joanne?"

"The very same," Mo gushed. "We've been flirting for weeks and she finally asked me out. I was beginning to think that she never would."

"You could've asked her," I told her. "It's a new day. Girls don't have to wait for girls to call them anymore."

"I know," she replied. "But I was getting mixed signals. I didn't want to risk it. But I have you to thank," she told me. *Me?*

"What did I do?" I asked her.

"You'll love this," Mo told me. "Turns out she thought you and I were together."

"*Together*, together?" I pressed.

"Yeah, but when she saw you with Rob, she figured you had to be straight. Or at least taken." I laughed 'til tears rolled down my cheeks.

"But I've been there with Coop and Rick, too," I reminded her.

"No," Mo said. "It was Robbie that convinced her." And it was, Robbie, that is. If only he didn't hate me. But this wasn't about me. Now it was Mo's turn at romance with Joanne and that was wonderful.

"Can you promise me one thing?" I asked Mo.

"Anything," she replied.

"Just promise you won't sign holiday cards 'Love, Mo & Jo' Okay? That would just be wrong. Please?"

Now it was Mo's turn to laugh. We hugged and laughed, and then she went back to work and I got on with it. I had a business to start and a life to live. I cleaned up, changed the sheets, and started a load of clothes. Stacked the dishwasher and made two trips to the trashcan and one to the recycling bin. Went for a long walk that afternoon, stocked up on groceries, and called Suze to share Mo's good news. Although the two of them had yet to meet, I had a feeling that they would get along well. I spent a couple of hours putting the finishing touches on my business plan, and finally scrambled some eggs and drank some juice. I was suddenly ravenous, so I followed up my meal with a huge dish of coffee ice cream.

Jag must have realized that I was back among the living, as he left me to do cat things after dinner. I read for a while, then watched the news before turning in. Just as I was starting to fall asleep, I felt Jagger's comforting presence as he joined me on the bed.

"Good boy," I told him. "You're my good boy. You miss him too, huh?" I took his silence for agreement. I finally fell asleep to the sound of his loud, contented purring. I would have to figure something out. Robbie back East and me here in Sedona? This was just not how it was meant to be.

CHAPTER 23

♫ Should I Stay or Should I Go? ♫

"Ummn, no. I guess not. No. Not really. Not at all," Rick was hesitant to come clean, to admit the truth. It was kind of fun to watch him squirm.

I had finally gotten up the nerve to ask Rick the question that had been plaguing me for months: Did you even remember me? I certainly had my doubts when I showed up unannounced at his job nearly seven months earlier. The poor guy had seemed genuinely confused. At the time, I wanted to blame the heat or that it was the end of a busy day that prevented him from recognizing me. Also, the fact that my bangs had grown out and I had gotten some sun on the drive out. But deep down, I really wasn't surprised by his response just now, when I finally asked him. I don't know if he made a habit of writing on his business cards or even if the note had been actually meant for me. I guess I never will. And that was fine with me.

"Hey Jackie?" I looked across the table at Rick. He was obviously uncomfortable, seeming to assume that I would be disappointed by his response. Okay, to be honest? It did sting just a little bit, but actually? I didn't really care. It was the first time that Rick and I had exchanged more than just a few words in passing since he got back last week from his extended stay in Cottonwood. He had called me that first night, but I was noncommittal when he told me he wanted to see me. I had finally heard from Robbie the day before and I think things were looking up. My ex had admitted that the thought of going back home after such a great reunion was really upsetting to him. But it looked like he had resolved himself to the situation and we were back on track. Towards what? I honestly have no idea. Being together, really together, would require a commitment and a cross-country move for one of us. As much as the idea of being back with Rob thrilled me, the thought of moving back to New England left me cold. Too many memories. Some good, but many of opportunities left unexplored. All of the things that I could've done, should have done, better or just differently. I didn't want to revisit the past. I doubted the new me would continue to thrive if I left Sedona. I was just glad to be here, knowing that Robbie was on my side, if not in my bed. It would have to be enough for now.

I had been avoiding Rick; there was no doubt about it. I finally agreed to see him but nixed the idea of getting together at either of our places, in favor of a more neutral location that would negate the likelihood that he would expect that we would end up in bed. That was how we happened to be sitting across the table from each other late in the afternoon at Caffe-Nation. It was Mo's day off and I knew that she and Joanne had gone to Phoenix together to some ritzy spa. The little café was pretty much deserted. Other than a part-time barista wiping down the counter, it was just the two of us.

I don't know that Rick's had a lot of experience being dumped, but that was the order of the day. The fact that he hadn't remembered me last summer made it easier to tell him that I was back with my ex. Kind of. But either way, I couldn't be with Rick, too. I just wasn't that kind of girl. All through high school and college, I had been faithful to whatever boyfriend I was with at the time. No doubling up like many of my friends.

Rick was cool. He understood and to be honest, didn't seem too broken up about the fact that we wouldn't be sleeping together or dating any longer.

"You were so nice to me when I came out here. I was such a mess. You must have been worried that I was some kind of psycho," I told him. Rick laughed at that.

"So why did you ask me out back then?" I asked him. It certainly hadn't been love at first sight. I suddenly had to know. Rick grinned. That same grin that would have just about done me in a few months back.

"You're kidding, right? You're just about the coolest, prettiest girl I've ever met. You just seemed so into it ... the move, the desert, that cat of yours. Just being around you, I don't know, it was just so easy. So good. I meet a lot of phony people, ya know? But not you. You're, I don't know. Authentic?" *Wow. Good answer.*

I threw out the 'I hope we can still be friends' olive branch, and I actually thought we could be. I know that I wanted to be. After the initial whirlwind, things between us had settled down. Way down. And we had never defined our relationship either. Several times, I got the distinct impression that he was seeing other women, okay, girls, but he was pretty discrete, and honestly, I didn't care all that much. Not really. I had never tried to stake my claim on him. He was beautiful to look at and uncomplicated as hell, but I had known better and I wanted more and it was not going to happen with Rick. As we said goodbye, he bent down and kissed me on the forehead. Easy enough to do, as he stood half a foot taller than me.

"I like you, Jackie," Rick said. "I hope you'll be happy. Rob's a lucky guy."

"I'll see you around, Rick," I promised and I would. He was a likable guy and Sedona was a small town, after all.

The next few weeks were kind of strange. Plans for the business were progressing and I had an open house scheduled for April 1. April Fool's Day. Maybe not the most auspicious of dates, but it was good timing and a Saturday, so I figured I would go with that.

I had hired an IT specialist who would start in a few weeks and I had the good fortune to recruit Joanne's younger sister as my receptionist/office manager. She had been downsized by a consulting firm in Phoenix and had recently made the move to be closer to her big sister. Amy was a real sweetheart, hard-working, funny, and she exuded such positive energy. I felt good about my choices in personnel as well as in real estate. I had negotiated a one-year lease on a central location in uptown Sedona. Robbie had given it his approval a few weeks back. There was already a roomy reception area in the front, along with two small offices and a unisex restroom. The back half of the building was unfinished, so I was drafting plans to build a partition creating two classrooms separated by a narrow hallway. I had decided that one of them would be more traditional and I would set it up theater style with long tables and chairs facing a podium, projector, and whiteboard. This would be the room I would use for most of the classes that I hoped to schedule. The other half of the new space would be set up like a conference room. I had been searching in every store and dusty garage that I could, for an eight-foot conference table. I wanted something spectacular, not just something I could pick up at Staples. It would be large enough to seat twelve to fourteen, and would be a great place to tape mock interviews and hold meetings. There was a small parking lot in the back, but being Uptown, I figured my clients would be used to parking on the street or would arrive on foot. All in all, it was an ideal location. So it was a busy time, but like I said, kind of strange. I felt vaguely unsettled most of the time. I would walk into a room and forget my reason for being there. I kept multiple lists and although I knew I was making progress, I still felt adrift. I spoke with Robbie almost daily and although most of our calls started out being business-related, we usually took a few moments just to chat. He ended each call with a warm goodbye.

"Love you, Jax."

"Me too," was what I said. "Love you more, Robbie," was what I thought. I knew I was giving off mixed signals. But he was cool. Things seem to have settled down for him at work and although he wasn't thrilled with the direction his agency was going, he was glad to have a couple of new high-profile accounts to work on. We always had so much to talk about, lots of news to share.

I had breakfast with Rick the week before, but that was about it. I had asked him if he was interested in the remodeling job at ENCORE, but he couldn't really give it the time it required as the tourist season was gearing up and he was again in heavy rotation. Mo and Joanne had been seeing a lot of each other and I was glad to see my friend so happy. I still visited the coffee shop almost daily, and had dinner with Mo every so often.

One night I invited her and her girlfriend over and spent the day cooking and preparing a feast. In deference to Mo,

Joanne turned down my offer of a glass of wine and the three of us dug into the bacon-wrapped shrimp and scallops I had prepared as a starter and we polished off a full pitcher of iced tea between us. We chattered away all evening and I learned that my girlfriend's new girlfriend had a wicked sense of humor and a big heart. She was funny and lovely and I was delighted to see how crazy they were about each other. I had never seen Mo so relaxed. So happy. We gorged on Caesar salad and lasagna and ended up being too full to do justice to the pastries that Mo had brought. It was a super evening and I got emails from each of them the next day thanking me. Sometimes friendships suffer when one of the friends began a new relationship, but I vowed not to let that happen with Mo and me. I had lost enough people I cared about and was determined not to lose any more.

I still celebrated Aloha Fridays, often with Coop. He had proven himself to be true connoisseur of Sedona take out, as well as an enthusiastic, actually hard-core patron of rock 'n' roll. He had heard from his daughter over the holidays and was talking about flying east to see her this spring. I was glad, as the more I got to know him, the more I realized how much he missed her.

So all in all, things were good for me and the people I cared about. I just couldn't shake the feeling that something was off. Robbie and I were doing well, but how long could we survive in no-man's land? We weren't together, but we were no longer apart either. Maybe I was taking on too much starting a business? After all, I would be paying two salaries out of my own savings for weeks, before we even opened our doors and who knows how long it would take to break even? I had no intention of ever turning a large profit, but I hoped that our revenues would be covering the expenses within a year. I wouldn't take a salary for now, but I wanted to generate enough cash to be confident that I could comfortably afford to pay for ENCORE's overhead each month. It was a fairly large undertaking, but I was certain that my projections were accurate and that I was on to something big. I remembered being at a marketing conference once and listening to Jeff Taylor, founder of Monster.com, the online job search site. He told a spellbound audience: 'The harder I worked, the luckier I got.' So I worked hard and tried to keep the nagging doubts and worries from slowing me down. I hoped I would get lucky professionally as well as in my personal life. ENCORE was all about second chances after all.

CHAPTER 24

♫ The Boys of Summer ♫

Sedona was getting into the summer season early, and I found it difficult to believe that I hadn't even been here a full year yet. My days were busy and my calendar was filling up fast. Ever since ENCORE's open house last month, I had been meeting so many people, including Joe, the advertising guy who was hosting today's cookout. He had shown up at the opening and asked a lot of really good questions about our plans and growth strategies. I thought he was trying to pitch us as a new client, but was thrilled when he offered to run a series of pro-bono workshops on advertising for fledgling business owners. It was exactly what I had been hoping for. We sat right down and penciled in a few dates and he promised to get a working outline of the content as well as copy points for our promotional materials to me later that week. The first session in the series had been held last Wednesday evening and the feedback was sensational. I was looking forward to a long and successful collaboration with Joe and other local professionals.

I was also looking forward to a few days with Rob. He had flown out for the opening last month and our relationship continued to chug along. Still not sure where we would end up, but I was definitely enjoying the ride. I was psyched when he offered to come out again. Claiming he had more frequent flyer miles and built-up vacation days than he knew what to do with, Robbie had once again flown directly to Sedona and when I met him at the airport yesterday, his greeting was as unreserved and enthusiastic as ever. He was happy to join me at the cookout that Joe and his wife Meg had planned. I knew I should be doing some valuable networking, making connections with the other guests, but for now I was content to sit on the chaise in the shade with Rob. And let him fetch me juicy drinks. The heat was intense.

Meg and Joe's five-year-old twin sons could not have been cuter. I watched them play with the family golden retriever and marveled at their boundless energy and the joy they seemed to express at every turn.

"Penny for your thoughts," Robbie teased as he sat down next to me, delivering a large glass of berry infused lemonade. I gulped down half of it since I was both thirsty and unwilling to admit how much the idea of having children was becoming appealing. Pushing that aside for now, I responded like the old me.

"Just wondering how long it would take you to get back with my drink," I countered. I leaned back against him to soften the sharp retort just a bit. It felt good, despite the heat, to rest against him and feel the stresses of the last few weeks slip away.

"Dry heat, my ass," I had told Suze over the phone the other day. "Over 90 degrees is too effin' hot, dry or not."

Meg ushered us all back inside for the evening meal. The AC was going full force and the change in temperature was welcome. The buffet spread was unreal. No burgers or chicken, the meal featured grilled tenderloin, a huge platter of cold cooked lobster with the shells already split, tortellini salad, grilled vegetables, and crusty bread. I filled my plate and having lost sight of Rob, shared a plushy sofa in the family room with a couple that lived nearby. He was a software engineer for an aerospace company in Phoenix who frequently worked from home. She was an attorney who used to work with Meg and, after I told them about my new business, she quickly offered to conduct a series of legal seminars for new business owners. *Yesss! I* logged her office number into my phone and promised to call her the following week to discuss logistics. Having met my business obligations for the day, I sat back, tore into my delicious meal and allowed the couple to entertain me with stories of their recent trip to the Far East. From my vantage point on the couch, I could see Rob and our host in the adjacent dining room with their heads together, deep in conversation.

When the availability of dessert was announced, I went back into the dining room and got in line to select a tiny éclair to accompany a giant cupcake that I soon learned tasted as good as it looked. I connected again with Rob and, shortly after the espresso and after-dinner cordials were put out, we said our goodbyes and left together. Just like a real couple.

"I like your friends," Rob enthused on the short drive back to the guest house. The rest of his visit flew by and before I knew it, Robbie was gone and I was back at work. Amy had been a great find, and in between keeping the reception area in order and greeting clients, she had been following up and contacting potential workshop leaders. I was having mixed feelings about Kevin, my other recent hire, however. His job description entailed developing policies and procedures for our daily operations and setting up the accounts and databases we would use to track revenues, expenses, and a calendar of projected courses. There was probably more than enough on his plate, but somehow, I had convinced Kevin that he would be a great workshop leader himself and had offered to pay him extra to develop sessions on topics of interest to our clients, like computer security and QuickBooks. Initially, he was not confident that he was suited for more than the behind-the-scene duties for which he was hired. But the lure of extra wages won out and Kevin told me that he was willing to give teaching a try. Most mornings he spent in the office next to mine, working on lesson plans and trying to create course objectives detailing the vast amount of computer knowledge circulating in his brain. Progress on his other daily duties was slow and I had to remind him several times that the classroom prep work needed to take place on his own time and that there was a lot of work that had to get done. I really did not enjoy ordering others around or micro-managing anyone and honestly, I found him to be less than receptive to my suggestions, even a bit intimidating. Lacking social skills, he grunted excuses and avoided eye contact with me. Other than a couple of daily check-ins, I found myself steering clear of him. I must lack the leadership gene. Either that or I'm just a big wuss.

I delivered a couple of training sessions myself on how to provide excellent customer service, and I had to admit that it felt great to be in front of a classroom again. The participants were a mixed group of local artisans, shop owners, and wait staff from area restaurants. I was delighted when I recognized a few of them, including Carla from my first meal with Rick nearly a year ago. She greeted me enthusiastically and even asked how my 'boyfriend' was. I explained that we were no longer together and agreed with her that we had been 'such a cute couple.' *Yikes.*

I spent a fair amount of time interviewing speakers on a wide variety of business-related topics and negotiating contracts with them. But most of my efforts were focused on marketing; filling seats and populating the early morning, lunchtime, evening, and Saturday morning sessions that we began offering. We offered everything from business essentials to recruiting and hiring tactics for business owners, to strategies for getting hired for those looking to change career fields. My sales tactics ran the gamut from starting a blog for area entrepreneurs and a Facebook page for job changers, to old school efforts like flyers, press releases, small display ads in the local Pennysaver, and giving radio interviews. I wanted to get the word out that ENCORE was a one-stop professional resource for the greater Sedona area. With phone traffic at twice the volume I had projected after the first three weeks, I instructed Amy to hire two part-timers. I put her in charge of scheduling their hours and providing on-the-job training. It was so rewarding when, through Mo, I learned that Amy had confided to her big sister that she saw real potential at ENCORE and that I was the 'best boss ever.'

Whenever time permitted, I brought in bagels or pizza for impromptu staff meetings at one end of the huge farmhouse-style table that had finally arrived. Kevin passed on most of the chatter, as he would usually come in, grab his share of food, and retreat back to his office, claiming to have too much work to do to sit around gabbing. Not exactly the team player I had been counting on.

The summer months were hectic, but I was enjoying every moment. Sundays I scheduled valuable me-time to hike, followed by a mani-pedi or a leisurely shopping trip. I tried to keep social engagements to a minimum, but made exceptions for Coop and Mo/Jo, of course Robbie, whenever he would visit. Jagger greeted me as enthusiastically as you could expect for a cat at the end of each day and sometimes, when I snuck home for a snack during the mid-afternoon lull as well. Even after I fed him and groomed him with the wire brush I had purchased, he would linger for a while. He was getting used to me working and being a latchkey cat.

I saw Rick on occasion around town, usually as he drove an eager group of tourists through the surface streets on route to the desert. He had even sent flowers on the day of the open house. Although he had RSVP'd in the affirmative, he was a no-show that day. I was touched by the gesture and if Robbie read the cheery note of congratulations enclosed, he didn't say a word.

In the midst of all the excitement, Edie decided at the last minute to squeeze in a quick visit. It was her first time in Sedona and we had a ball! I brought her to all my favorite shops and restaurants and she even joined me on my morning hike on each of the four days she was here. I introduced her to Mo and they hit it off immediately. Even Coop got on board, inviting us for dinner on Edie's third night in town. I was curious, as I had had never seen him do any cooking or entertaining, save for a beer and snacks on the deck. But after meeting Edie, he apparently decided to break out the good china and had an amazing four course meal catered and served in his formal dining room.

"I didn't even know he had plates," I confided to Edie.

"Hush, Jax. He's adorable." was her quick reply. *Hmmm.* Apparently, it was a mutual attraction, as I was witness to my former stepmother-in-law doing the walk of shame at dawn the next morning. Hey, two consenting adults, right? I wasn't sure if I should say anything about what transpired, but I needn't have worried. In her usual straightforward way, Edie came right out with it. When I asked her how she wanted to spend her last evening in town, she was very emphatic. An early dinner at Oaxaca for the two of us, followed by a nightcap and an evening in with Coop.

"Life's short, Dollface," she reminded me with a wink as she grabbed a shawl and prepared to stroll across the patio later that evening. So true. Edie and Coop. Go figure.

So I was going 'bout my business and doing fine. Life was good. And then all hell broke loose, and it was hard to find anything that was even remotely good. The proverbial shit hit the fan. The dog days of summer had officially begun.

CHAPTER 25

♫ I Still Haven't Found What I'm Looking For ♫

"No, really, I'm fine." For the second time in only twenty minutes, I tried to reassure the concerned flight attendant, that I was. Fine. But I wasn't. Not at all. I was trying to relax, but having a hard time getting comfortable. Everything that had transpired over the past several days had me convinced that I was a lousy friend. I was a crappy girlfriend. I had created a monster. I was a home wrecker. I was going to fail at my business venture after less than two months. I would likely be homeless soon. *Yeah, all that.*

"Okay, hon. But you let me know if I can get you somethin', okay?" Hon? Shades of Claire. She had always called me that. Relying on the kindness of strangers had never been a practice that I put much stock in, but the care that 'Joan', now that I could read her name tag, had shown me ever since I boarded the return flight home was a welcome relief. I vowed to write a letter to the airlines once I landed, expressing my gratitude for their brilliance in recruiting an amazing employee like … Joan. Yes, I would. Tears welled up in my eyes.

"Maybe just some tea? Hot tea?" I ventured.

"You got it, hon. Coming right up." Joan was on a mission and returned shortly with an overloaded tray containing a thermos of hot water, an assortment of teas, and sweeteners, a small jug of milk, a plate of sliced lemons, and a teacup and saucer. Oh, and a whole lot of cookies and biscuits. I thanked her warmly and again told her I was fine. Over the next half hour, I sipped Earl Grey and dunked cookies. I thought about my crappy life and wondered what I would do to make things better. It was too exhausting to contemplate. Everything was falling apart.

First off, Suze. Aarrgghh. I had flown back to Massachusetts on the spur of the moment and under some duress, in order to attend a dinner honoring her achievements in the local business community. She had told me several weeks ago that the local Chamber of Commerce had named her 'Woman of the Year' in recognition of her accomplishments. It was a big honor and I was thrilled for her. I immediately sent a huge fruit arrangement complete with white chocolate covered strawberries (her favorite) to her office, knowing she wasn't big on flowers. She had mentioned that there would be a dinner as well, but as I was up to my eyeballs starting my own business venture and was thousands of miles away, it didn't really occur to me that I would be expected to attend. She had plenty of family and business associates that would be there to support her that night. My support would be more of the virtual variety. Anyhow, we were talking last week and she casually asked me what my travel plans were. Come to find out, she had assumed that I was planning to attend the dinner and would have communicated my travel arrangements with her husband to surprise me. I confessed that I had not been planning to attend and that no such communication had occurred with her husband. Well, apparently, I was the worst friend ever, and her husband was a jerk for dropping the ball. I reached these conclusions after she shared her feelings quite explicitly before hanging up on me. Attempts to call her back that night were futile, so I made my flight reservations and emailed a copy of my itinerary to her the next morning. I would be arriving the day of the dinner and staying for two nights. It was a long trip to make for such a short stay, but I couldn't justify staying any longer on such short notice with everything else that was going on. Suze was somewhat mollified, but remained annoyed that I hadn't originally planned to be there for her. I was a little surprised that my presence meant that much to her, but I guess it wasn't all that unexpected. Suze was kind of a stickler for protocol and appearances and had very high expectations of the key people in her life. *Okay. I suck.*

Everything was crashing at ENCORE as well. Buoyed by the self-confidence gained from hosting a couple of successful seminars, Kevin was becoming a real diva. Suddenly he was way too busy to do the more mundane duties that went with his job and tried to pawn them off on Amy. Poor Amy was swamped and since one of the part-timers had not worked out, she was putting in lots of extra hours already. Essentially a people-pleaser and a middle child, she tried to keep the peace, cover for Kevin, and pick up the extra work, but things had been falling through the cracks. The training room was overbooked on two occasions causing unhappy seminar leaders and lots of confused clients. Bills weren't getting paid, and revenue wasn't coming in, as our clients' credit cards weren't being charged for the sessions they attended. Joe, my advertising go-to guy, confessed that he had waited on hold for ten minutes only to be disconnected when he called back.

"I was just trying to find out how many folks to expect at that night's session," he told me. That was the sort of thing that Kevin had assured me that we would be able to access on our intranet site, but it wasn't up and running as of yet. To make matters worse, Amy told me that she and her sister were contemplating moving together back to Phoenix in the wake of Joanne's recent breakup with Mo. Yeah, they broke up and no one was sure why. Mo was tightlipped on whatever had transpired between them. Kevin stormed off after I asked him the status of the website he had been working on and disappeared for the rest of the day. My frantic calls to his cell phone went straight through to voicemail.

But wait, there's more. As I was driving to the airport two days ago to travel back East despite the problems unresolved at work, Rick called me to apologize. Puzzled, I asked him "What for?" and he told me that Coop had admitted to him that his daughter was talking about moving to Sedona and wanted to take her dad up on his original offer to occupy the guest house. Rick felt responsible for originally suggesting that I rent from Coop in the first place.

"But I live there," I sputtered. "She had her chance." Rick had assumed that Coop had talked to me, but to be honest, with all of the drama at work and preparing for my hasty trip, my communication with my landlord had been minimal. I honestly wasn't sure how he and Edie had left things and I didn't want to open up a can of worms, as it were. I only had taken a moment to confirm that Coop would look after Jag for me while I was gone.

"Why'd he tell you?" I asked Rick.

"Oh, I thought you knew," he admitted. "I used to be married to her." *What?*

"You were married to Coop's daughter?" *How did I not know this?*

"Yeah," Rick was sheepish. "Katie and I were married for a couple years, but it didn't work out," he admitted. Oh hell, no. I was getting way too old for this kind of crap. I told Rick to tell Coop to tell Katie that if she really wanted it, I would move out, but I begged to be allowed to stay 'til the end of the summer. I was already at the airport by this point, so I told Rick I would talk to him later. Much later, I vowed.

Things continued to get worse. After a long day of travel and airport delays, no one was there to meet my flight. I had assumed that between Rob and Suze, they would have worked out the logistics, but I was wrong. I waited around like an idiot until it was quite clear that I was on my own. Suze was getting her hair done when I called her and Robbie was driving back from Boston that evening. Fuming, I took a cab to the inn that visiting professors at my former college used to frequent. It was the only place I could think of. And I had worried that Suze and Rob would fight over me and where I would stay. I planned to spend the first night with Suze and the next day and evening with my ex, but apparently had never communicated this with either of them. So after a hasty shower and the realization that I was in possession of not a single hair product, I threw on a dress that was wrinkled beyond repair, then called another cab to bring me to the dinner. On top of last minute airfare, I figured I could have taken a really nice spa vacation for half of what I had already spent just to get to the damned dinner.

When I arrived at the banquet hall, there was a ticket left in my name, but it was for a table by the kitchen apparently reserved for stragglers and guests that didn't fit anywhere else. If Robbie had been there with me, we would have laughed and turned being assigned to the 'weird cousin's table' into something more memorable. But he wasn't and I didn't. I silently worked my way through a wilted salad and the rubber chicken entrée. Not sure if I really had the right to be furious for such poor treatment, I settled for mildly annoyed and rebuffed attempts at conversation by my #19 tablemates. I pouted in the ladies' room and when I returned, my plate had been cleared, but unlike the other inhabitants of Table 19, there was no dessert left for me. Damn, and it actually looked good, too. Was that a caramel drizzle?

In her acceptance speech, Suze thanked everyone for being there and mentioned several people by name. My name and that of her husband were not among them. Oh well. I finally decided to be the bigger person and approached her at the head table at the end of the evening. Suze was gracious, but reserved, and after being snubbed by most of her family members in attendance, I told everyone good night and slunk off to the lobby to call a cab. *What a shit show.* I didn't think I could feel much worse. Wrong again.

"Wait, Jackie," Suze's husband stopped me. I turned, hoping that he was going to offer me a ride back to my hotel or something, but no.

"Thanks," he said sarcastically. "She's blaming me for not making your travel arrangements," he fumed. What a douche! Too stunned to reply, I turned on my heel and stomped out, threw the cab driver a $20 bill for an $11 fare a short time later and entered the hotel lobby. I briefly considered stopping at the bar to drown my sorrows, but decided to get change for candy from the vending machine I had spied earlier. *Three Musketeers* to the rescue.

"Jackie?" I heard a familiar voice and turned to find Robbie right behind me. For about the first time in recorded history, I was less than happy to see him.

"How did you know I was here?" I asked in amazement. Apparently, he had called around when he got home from his trip that evening and found that I had checked in earlier.

"Only the third place I tried," he told me, sounding quite pleased with his accomplishment.

"I thought I would see you tomorrow," I pleaded weakly. "It's been a real crap day and I'm feeling really lousy." I really was. I was starting to feel the aches and pains associated with a flu bug and my head had been pounding all night. Chocolate, Tylenol PM, and a good night's sleep were in order, but what to do about Rob? He had to be back in Boston first thing in the morning and had only made the round trip in order to spend a few hours with me. Normally I would have been thrilled at the thought of time alone with Rob. But not tonight. I blamed fatigue and feeling crappy and almost convinced both of us that whatever bug was ailing me was probably of the contagious variety. I tried to console him by agreeing to postpone my return flight by another day in order to spend some quality time with him. But I know he was hurt and pissed at me when he left a few minutes later without a hug or kiss.

After a quick stop at the vending machine, I let myself into my room and flopped onto the king-sized bed. My message light was blinking and after listening to an hours-old message left by my ex-husband, telling me that he was on his way over, I heard the voice of my oldest and best friend. Suze had left a message asking me to call her back as soon as I got in, but it was too late to talk that night. I was exhausted and still pissed by her shabby treatment of me earlier that evening.

I just wanted this lousy day to be over. Feeling feverish and smeared with chocolate, I fell into a troubled sleep.

I awoke hours later feeling much worse and called down to room service for soup and tea. Everything hurt. I was sore all over and still felt feverish. Hoping for chicken noodle, I was more than a little grossed out that the soup *du jour* was broccoli cheddar. I sipped my tea and decided to check my cell for messages. I had several. Coop, Mo, Amy, Kevin, and Rick had each called with a variety of concerns and complaints. Coop was apologetic.

"I told Rick not to call you. That I would deal with it myself. Damn busybody," he vented. "Don't worry," he concluded. "We'll work something out." I thanked him for being so sweet and told him I would see him soon. And to hug Jagger for me.

When I returned her call next, Mo wanted me to know that she and Joanne were talking again and that reports of Joanne's move back to Phoenix were greatly exaggerated. Other than that, she made it clear that she did not want to talk about it anymore. And to have a safe trip. Next, Amy told me that she would be there for me, one way or another, and to have a good time with all of my friends back home. *Uh huh.* Then Kevin reported that he wanted to renegotiate his compensation package, as his responsibilities were much greater than he had been led to believe. So, he was capable of speaking in full sentences. *Jerk.* I mumbled something about how I was expecting him to continue on with his duties while we sorted things out and that I would see him later in the week. By the time I talked to Rick, I was shaky and thoroughly exhausted. He cautioned me to not say anything about Katie to Coop, as his daughter's brief marriage was a real sore subject for him. I finally begged off and turned my phone on vibrate. Then I shoved it into my overnight bag. I was done. This was, apparently, my life, ladies and gentlemen.

I decided to face all these problems head-on. But first, I needed more sleep. I switched to a late afternoon flight back to Phoenix and arranged for a late checkout and a cab to the airport. Before succumbing to sleep, I asked for a two pm wakeup call and promptly passed out. By the time Robbie called to ask what I wanted to do that night, I was boarding my flight and it was *his* turn to hang up on me. Or maybe we just got disconnected. *Yeah, right.*

So this is what I was dealing with as I drank my tea and dunked my cookies. I slept for a few hours on the plane, but a delayed landing caused me to miss my connecting flight to Sedona. As it was the last flight of the night, the airline put me up in a hotel adjacent to the airport. I crashed there and slept for twelve straight hours. Feeling shaky but a bit more in control, I landed back in Sedona midday, drove home, cuddled with Jag, and moped. I poked around in the fridge and tossed out some fruit that had spoiled. Nothing looked good. I flipped through some CDs and scanned my IPod. Nothing sounded good. I spent a very productive hour cleaning out my email's spam filter. The various Canadian pharmacies, someone named Hipster, and all the sex-crazed creepers out there would have to find someone else to pick on besides me. Feeling a tiny sense of having accomplished something, anything, I curled up with a book for a while then I slept until I couldn't sleep any longer. Since it was now three am on a Sunday, there was little I could do to save my business and repair my relationships right then. I found a pint of mocha fudge in the freezer and sprawled on my sofa, channel surfing and trying to come up with a plan. I honestly had no clue where to begin. *Crap.*

CHAPTER 26

♫ Nothing Compares 2 U ♫

"Fire his ass."

"Really?"

"Yeah, Jax. Do it. The little turd." I smiled at the image I had of my sweet former stepmother-in-law pacing back and forth and getting all worked up. She was so little and so feisty. I just loved her.

"You haven't lost your sassy skills, Edie. No way. Still got'em."

"You could use a little sass yourself, Sister," was her immediate reply.

"Me?" I questioned. "What do you mean? I'm plenty sassy."

"Then stop letting everyone, including my handsome stepson, walk all over you," she countered. *Ouch, that hurt.* But I should have known what I was in for when I called her and asked for her advice. Edie was a straight shooter and pulled no punches. I had waited around and kept my distance from everyone for a few days after I returned from my trip back east. I hoped that things would settle down, without any real action on my part. And things had calmed down a bit, I had to admit. At least no one was hanging up on me. Or yelling at me. Of course, no one was really talking to me either. Things were far from perfect. I was miserable at work and I avoided contact with my staff. I actually pretended to be talking on the phone when Amy tried to talk to me on my first day back. I held up a finger and mouthed, "Sorry, this is important," but I'm sure she knew. I feared that my fledgling business was on the verge of imploding. I dodged both Coop and Mo, and I stressed out when I thought about Suze. My days were long and miserable and at night, I was dreaming about Robbie. Every night. Suddenly I'm a dreamer. And the dreams? I remember them quite vividly and blushed whenever I did. I wished I could sext him or something but we weren't even talking. *Crap.*

"I'm serious, Jax. You figure out what you want and you ask for it. Hell, you demand it. You're worth it. Don't waste your time on anyone who doesn't see that," Edie advised. Pretty strong advice from someone who had put up with a cheating cad like Rob Senior for all those years. But I had to admit, the woman knew her stuff. She had it going on. Her home was paid for, she was quite comfortable, and she spent her time on volunteer work, lunching with her friends, daily ocean swims, and tooling around town in a late model red convertible. When she had been out to visit last month, she confided that she had a *friend t*o spend quality time with. A little younger. They had met playing tennis. He was a 'darling', according to Edie.

"What about Coop?" I asked her now. *'Don't hurt him,'* I begged silently.

"He's called me several times since I got back. I think he wants to come and visit me," she told me and sounded very happy about the idea. Apparently, they had really connected. If the best revenge is living well, Edie was the proof.

Sounded good to me. I would listen to her and see what advice she had for me.

"Kick that tour guide to the curb," she told me. "You deserve more." Okay, I had already done that. Then she advised me to call Suze and tell her that I loved her. That I had screwed up. That I was her oldest friend and to give me a break. And then to give her a little space. She suggested an equally direct approach with Coop.

"You can't hide from him forever," she reasoned. "Invite him over for coffee. Tell him you love living there, but you understand that family comes first. Ask him what's going on with his daughter and then deal with it. Once you know, you can make your plans. It's the not knowing that's killing you." I had to admit that that she made a lot of sense. And she certainly had an insight into the man that I would never have. She suggested that I give Mo space as well, but to reach out and let her know that I was there for her. As far as ENCORE went, it was simple. March in there as soon as we hung up. Offer Amy a raise provided she would stay and then fire Kevin.

"It's still during the first ninety days. You don't need to give him a reason, just show him the door. You could get him on treason or insubordination or whatever, but why bother? Just tell him that it's not working out and you'll pay him 'til the end of the week, but that he needs to leave today."

"But it's already Thursday," I told her.

"All the better," was her response. "Then sit down with Amy and make a list of every dollar you have coming to you and send out the bills. Reach out to all your teachers."

"Facilitators," I corrected her.

"Whatever. Invite them in, get a bunch of pizzas or donuts, and make peace. Admit that things got out of hand and tell them you'll do everything in your power to fix it.

Show them how committed you are, and they'll work with you. You can't fail."

There was one piece of advice she had left out. One problem that there was no easy fix for. Robbie. What should I do about Robbie?

"Oh, darling. You're going to need to work that out yourself," she cautioned, "I can't tell you what you need to do." To her credit, she had tried to previously. She had argued unsuccessfully with both Robbie and me when we told her that we were splitting up nearly three years earlier.

"Fight for him, Jax. Don't give up on him," she had begged. But I didn't know how to fight back then and I'm honestly not sure if I've learned how in the time since. So there I was, still struggling to stay afloat.

"But Edie," I moaned. "He hates me."

"No Jax, he loves you. And I know you love him. But you've got to tell him. Tell him what you want." But that was part of the problem. I didn't know what I wanted. Well, actually I knew *what* I wanted, just not *how* to make it work. I wanted Rob and I wanted to run a successful business and I wanted to be happy. Is that too much to ask? Why was this *sooo* difficult?

But meanwhile I had problems even more pressing to solve and fences to mend as well. So I buckled down and I followed all of Edie's advice and I could see it working. Things were starting to improve. And contrary to my Whack-A-Mole theory of life, new problems did not emerge. At least not right away. I was really grateful for the reprieve. Coop assured me that I had a place to live for as long as I wanted. That his daughter Katie made noises about wanting to move in every so often. That if she ever actually showed up in town, he would find her a place to stay.

"Sedona's her green grass, you know. It's always better somewhere else. When she's tired of dealing with the everyday issues we all have to face, she starts to think she can solve everything by moving here. As if that would solve everything. Can you imagine?" *Yes, yes I can.* About her short-lived marriage to Rick, all he would say was this:

"I felt bad for Rick when she left him like that. He tried to make things work, he really did. But Katie never learned to trust him or anyone for that matter. That's on me," he admitted. Katie had left Rick? I hadn't imagined that. I decided to give Rick a break. He had been dumped and that must have hurt. Maybe that was why he had never fessed up to his ex's identity. Poor guy.

I sent a funny BFF card to Suze, then followed up with a call. I told her just what Edie had recommended that I tell her and she didn't hang up. We left things open. I told her to give me a call whenever and that I loved her. I know she'll come around. Mo and Joanne are working things out and are looking to move in together. Amy was more than welcome to live with them, and she agreed to join in their search for the perfect place to set up house.

I fired Kevin the next day. Told him I would pay him for an extra week then watched him pack up a few things off his desk and leave in a huff. *Good riddance.* Amy and I immediately got busy changing passwords on all of the computer files and even changed the locks. I didn't think my former employee was capable or even interested in any kind of retribution, but you can't be too sure, I reasoned. We buckled down and mailed out invoices to all the workshop participants from the last few weeks. Amy had been keeping good records. I couldn't be sure, but it looked like we would cover our expenses for the month even if only half of them paid up. We activated the online registration forms that Kevin had neglected, ensuring that we would get the funds up front from now on. I made personal calls to all of the seminar facilitators and several of them I visited in person. I decided to one-up Edie, and with Coop's approval, invited them over for cocktails on the patio at home. I made sure to connect with each of them and ask them to give ENCORE an encore. *Yeah, I said it.* And it worked. They all signed on. I was back in business.

I felt more energetic than I had in weeks. Things were back on track. Well, most things. I started hiking again just about every day. As I was sleeping more soundly, my 'sex with the ex' dreams ended and I mourned their loss. I decided that I needed to initiate the real thing. A tryst was definitely in order.

I figured a neutral, somewhat central location was just the thing. Deciding that the Windy City was a perfect place to heat things back up, I texted Robbie. I offered to make all the arrangements; all he had to do was to board the flight. And he did. We had an amazing time together and the neutral location was aphrodisiacal. If that is not a real word, you get my drift, right? At the end of the long weekend, we each flew back to our respective home bases with a promise for a repeat performance and soon. Life got back to the new normal for a while, but the questions remained. What the hell was I really doing out here and why was I doing it alone?

CHAPTER 27

♫ Suddenly I See ♫

I woke up early and knew instantly that something was up. After almost three years of living alone, it's amazing how quickly you get so used to having someone in bed with you. Robbie had been staying with me for nearly a week and I have got to tell you, it was pretty fabulous. Kind of like our early days together but even better. Sweeter. Even more special. When he had offered to fly out again, I immediately agreed and began to plan a fun-filled time with day trips. I made a list of all of the restaurants, shops, and galleries that I'd been meaning to get to for the past year. Well, we didn't cross everything off my list. Barely made a dent, if you must know. Spent a lot of time hiking and talking, and even more time in bed. Like yesterday, we woke up early, greeted the day with some very enthusiastic lovemaking, showered together, and walked to Caffe-Nation for lattes. Visited with Mo. Meandered about, moseyed, window shopped. Robbie bought me a pair of silver and coral hoop earrings. I have been unjustly accused in the past of being hard to shop for. But I'm really not. I am an equal opportunity gift receiver. You can buy me just about anything—jewelry, scarves, bags, books … I'm easy. We went back to the guest house, played with Jagger, and then took a long hike. Another shower then drove to Oaxaca for an amazing dinner. Tired and full, we came back and watched TV, cuddling on the couch with Jagger. Turned in early and fell asleep in each other's arms. Perfect. Couldn't be better.

But here I was seven or eight hours later, still in bed, but alone. *Hmmm.* I modestly covered up in a robe. Even at my fighting weight, I lacked the confidence to stride around naked. Gravity, you know. Plus, I had recently put on a few pounds. Robbie said I looked great, but old insecurities die hard. Terrycloth was my new best friend.

I padded barefoot into the living room and found the object of my affection. Both of them. Robbie was reclining on the couch with his feet up on the coffee table. Jagger was stretched out and balanced on Robbie's legs. Robbie looked lost in thought. Jagger was in a deep sleep.

"Hey, there's my boys," I said lightly. "How're you doing?" Robbie looked up.

"Hey, grab some coffee and join me, okay?" *Yikes.* What was up?

"Refill?" I offered.

"No I'm good," he replied. I hurried to the kitchen and filled my mug.

"Here I am," I said brightly, sitting down on the couch next to Robbie. Careful not to spill my coffee and not wanting to disturb His Royal Highness, I perched gingerly on the edge of my seat.

"So what's up?" I finally got up the nerve to ask.

"Jax," Robbie's eyes looked sad and were rimmed with red. *Were those tears? Oh shit. Danger, danger.* "This isn't working." *Oh no.*

"What, us?"

"No, this. Flying back and forth."

"Do you want me to come out your way next time? I could …"

"No, that's not it."

"Then what?" Silence. "I don't know what you want." *Tell me, please.*

"I want it all, okay?" *That wasn't what I was expecting.*

"All?"

"Yeah all. All of you, all the time." My flip retort died on my lips. No time for a double entendre. *Oh my God. I think he means it.*

"I love you, Jax, and I know you love me. I have an opportunity that I want to tell you about but I gotta know. Are you in?"

"In?" God, I was having a hard time keeping up.

"Pick me, Jax. Choose me. Dump him, I don't care. I love you, pick me."

I resisted the urge to tease him that his plea was straight out of a *Grey's Anatomy* script. I looked at his handsome face and grasped his hands in mine. Suddenly, I knew. I could see it all so clearly. The only way that my life made any sense at all was if Robbie was in it. All the way in.

"I do love you, Rob. I'm in." *Of course I am.*

"I have a chance to buy into an agency here. Partner with Joe, remember him?"

Remember him? I had introduced him to Robbie myself. What was going on?

"We hit it off, Jax. Really. He wants to expand, move further into social media … I've even met with some of his clients."

"You what? When?"

"The other morning when you went into the office? I told you I was going for coffee and I did, just not alone."

"Sneaky, Rob, very sneaky."

"I know, but I had to make sure that if you *were* on board, I'd have something. A way to support us."

Images of workaholic Robbie filtered through my head. Client dinners, early morning breakfast meetings, Saturdays at the office…. Combined with my quest for tenure, that's what broke us up the first time, wasn't it?

"It'll be different this time, Jax." God, he always could read my mind. "I'm different. I'd be a partner—an equal. And you know Joe. He works hard, but he's a family man, right?" I pictured Meg and their two little boys. I nodded.

"Yes, he is. So how would this work? I don't really get it."

"We've assessed the value of the company. I'll be making an initial investment then I'll take a smaller cut for a year or so until we're even. The money will allow us to take on more space and more associates, upgrade the technology. We'll be state-of-the-art Jax. It'll be epic. We complement each other perfectly. Joe is good with the numbers and I'm good with clients and we're both pretty creative … we're perfect together."

I leaned in and Robbie circled me in his arms.

"No, we're perfect together," I whispered into his ear. Annoyed with all the talk and movement and sensing that shenanigans were likely to commence, Jagger jumped up, stalked across the room, and took up a new post on the rug.

"Sorry, Jag," we both said in perfect unison. Robbie laughed.

"We're gonna be one of those couples, Jax. You know the ones. They talk to each other through their pets. Like 'Jag, tell Mom that lunch is ready.'"

I chimed in with "Jag, tell Daddy he's an idiot. But I love him. Tell him, Jag. I love him. I always have and I always will." Visions of us growing old together made me smile, but something was still troubling me.

"Rob, before you said dump him, you meant Rick?" He looked surprised.

"Yeah, why is there someone else?"

"Oh God, no. There's no one … well, except maybe Coop." At Rob's startled look, I quickly added, "Kidding. But no, Rick isn't in the picture. He never really was. I haven't seen him in weeks. I was looking for something. I thought it was him. But it was bigger than that. I needed to change. To know that I could. You know it, right? It's magical here. I was meant to come here. I just thought I needed a Mr. Right or whatever for it to make sense."

"I'm Mr. Right," Robbie interjected. I had to agree. When he's right, he's right.

"I guess the second time's the charm," I added. "Hey Rob?"

"Yeah, Jax?"

"You really need to kiss me. You've gotten awfully stingy with those kisses, Mister," I laughed. And Robbie kissed me again and again and again. I felt so happy, *this* was my ever after. It took us awhile and we hit a bumpy detour. But we were back. And it was good. It was damn good.

CHAPTER 28

♫ I Can't Tell You Why ♫

By the time I realized what was happening, it was too late. Not that I would've done anything differently, I mean, it was surprising, unexpected, inexplicable even. But it was good. And Robbie was over the moon. About everything. He gave his notice at the agency and finalized the financial arrangements with his new partner, Joe. With no time to drive out, everything he owned would be shipped here, including his car and he would fly out the following week. I had been exceptionally busy over the last several weeks and blamed my exhaustion on the ramped-up activity level. ENCORE was doing well. Real well. We've been talking about opening a second location (ENCORE ENCORE?) up in Flagstaff. Mo had told me that she wanted to run it. She and Joanne were looking to buy a place together, and their money would go a lot further outside of town. They made a really cute couple. No one ever called them 'Mo & Jo', except me, behind their backs. Rick had started dating Chrissy from work and seemed happy. He's a good guy and he deserves to be happy. It was a little weird, but Robbie didn't choke when I said we should get together with them sometime. He didn't exactly get out a calendar either, but hey, it's a small town, you know? Bound to happen, sooner or later. I tried take long walks whenever I felt up to it, and of course, I talked to Robbie every day, sometimes two or three times. We had so much to talk about, so many plans to make. Where to live for one. We decided to stay in Coop's guesthouse for a few more months and keep Rob's stuff in storage when it arrived. That would give Robbie a chance to get the lay of the land and settle in to his new position. He and Joe were like kids, planning and plotting. It was wonderful to see him so happy and so excited.

I'd pretty much decided on the neighborhood I wanted us to be in. Near Coop. I figured we would end up in a 3/2—that's three bedrooms and two bathrooms, I learned, but I was flexible. Visions of our too-big first house haunted me. I was going for cozy this time around. But a good-sized yard, that was a definite, a given as we were talking about getting a dog. Jag would have to get used to sharing us soon anyway and I mean, every kid should grow up with a dog, right? #andbabymakesthree

JACKIE'S PLAYLIST

SONG   ARTIST

Blowin' In the Wind: *Bob Dylan*

Running on Empty: *Jackson Browne*

In My Life: *The Beatles*

Into the Mystic: *Van Morrison*

The Way We Were: *Barbra Streisand*

Time for Me to Fly: *REO Speedwagon*

Hello It's Me: *Todd Rundgren*

Gimme Shelter: *The Rolling Stones*

It's Aloha Friday: *Kimo Kahoano*

I Heard it Through the Grapevine: *Marvin Gaye*

Night Moves: *Bob Seger*

Moves Like Jagger: *Maroon 5*

What I Need is a Good Defense: *Fiona Apple*

American Woman: *The Guess Who*

You Can't Always Get What You Want:
The Rolling Stones

The Heart of the Matter: *Don Henley*

I am Barely Breathing: *Duncan Sheik*

Key West Intermezzo: *John Mellencamp*

Gail Ward Olmsted

Losing My Religion: *R.E.M.*
You're My Home: *Billy Joel*
Should I Stay or Should I Go?: *The Clash*
The Boys of Summer: *Don Henley*
I Still Haven't Found What I'm Looking For: *U2*
Nothing Compares 2 U: *Sinead O'Connor*
Suddenly I See: *KT Tunstall*
I Can't Tell You Why: *The Eagles*

Did you enjoy *Jeep Tour*? I hope so, but I would love to hear from you either way. You can find me on Facebook (Gail Olmsted Author) on Twitter @gwolmsted or email gwolmsted@gmail.com I hope that you will take the time to post a review on Amazon or a rating on Goodreads. Authors live and die by these reviews, so please give some feedback. It is much appreciated!

Check out my other titles: www.GailOlmsted.com

Guessing at Normal ~ Driving on the Left Second Guessing ~ Landscape of a Marriage

Want to hear more of Jackie Sullivan's story? Fast forward 20 years and she and Rob have a daughter graduating from college. Here's the first chapter of *Driving on the Left* for your enjoyment!

Best for now,

Gail

Driving on the Left

CHAPTER ONE

Jackie

No matter how often you travel, let's face it: packing is a real pain in the ass. It's always a struggle—what to pack and how much of it. Easy enough to over-pack, that's for sure. But then you're stuck dragging everything around the whole time you're gone, and you have no room in your luggage for souvenirs and gifts. Under-packing is also pretty easy, I guess. "If I really need it, I can get it there" could be an effective approach, depending on where you are headed.

My best friend, Suze, sent me a link a few years back chock full of packing tips. I printed it out and promptly lost it, but from what I can remember, it was mostly commonsense advice: roll your T-shirts, stuff corners with socks, pick items that are multi-use, blah, blah, blah. Unfortunately, common sense is in short supply this afternoon. My brain is mush, and my bedroom looks like it was hit by a tornado.

Tomorrow morning, my daughter Rebecca and I are flying to Ireland! We will be there for three weeks. She graduated from college earlier this month, and we're celebrating.

My husband Rob was scheduled to go with us, but his business partner needed an emergency appendectomy and will be out of commission for at least another week. They own the largest advertising agency here in the northern Verde Valley of Arizona, and there is just too much going on for both of them to be out of the office at the same time. I hope Rob can join us fairly soon. I will miss the hell out of him, but maybe a little time apart is what we need right now. It's been really tense around here lately.

What I'm getting ready for was supposed to be a relaxing vacation, but I've got to do some serious soul-searching over the next couple of weeks. Rob wants an answer, and I promised him one. Why I am convinced that the solution to our problem will come to me in a foreign country, when I haven't been able to figure it out here at home over the last several weeks? Well, that's beyond me. But I live in hope. The future of my marriage depends on it.

The last couple of weeks have been busier than usual, tying up loose ends at work and finalizing travel arrangements. Even though Amy, my business partner, is more than capable of running Encore without me, I'm still a little anxious about leaving.

We are going to take a guided tour of Ireland, but not the kind of tour bus that you are probably thinking of. It's more of a van, and there will only be eight or ten of us, plus the tour guide. Becca found it online. It promises to take us "off the beaten track to discover the real Ireland." A chance to see some amazing sights, hit all the top attractions, have our own tour guide, and not be saddled with fifty or sixty other travelers? Sounds good to me.

Wait, are you thinking about that other time I took a guided tour…? My girlfriend Suze has been cracking up about this upcoming Ireland trip ever since I told her about it. And when I mentioned that Rob was not going to be able to join us at first…. Well, let's just say she had a field day. Rob's ex-stepmother joined in to laugh, as well. Typical Edie.

"Be careful, doll face," she said. "What with your track record..."

Yeah, simply hilarious. My *track record*? It's not exactly common knowledge. Many of my current friends, employees, and clients have no idea what first brought me to Sedona more than two decades ago. But Rob knows, of course. Even Becca has heard that her sedate, middle-aged mom had a romantic fling with a sexy tour guide, sandwiched between two marriages to her father.

Okay, let's back up. Here's the story, starting back nearly twenty-four years ago in Massachusetts…

———————

My marriage to Rob had ended in divorce, but we were still romantically involved. Well, *sexually* involved, that is. Long story, but one for a different day.

I was a marketing professor at the time, on the tenure track at a local college. A couple of my colleagues and I went out to Phoenix to attend a conference. It was a totally forgettable few days, but we had decided beforehand to tack on some time at the end and drive a couple of hours north to Sedona. My co-worker Kate had heard Sedona was a great place to visit, so we booked a triple room for two nights and headed up there for a little R and R.

Kate had heard right. Sedona *is* spectacular. Red rocks, bright blue skies, vistas galore. For our one full day in town, we scheduled a Jeep tour of the desert. Kate packed her camera, and the three of us showed up at the appointed time, ready to be amazed. Rick, our tour guide, was also pretty spectacular, if you like tall, bronzed, blond hunks, that is. And I did.

We had a really great day exploring the desert. Rick was knowledgeable, entertaining, and kind of flirty. At the end of the tour, he gave me his number, scribbled on the back of one of his business cards. *Call me,* it read.

I laughed it off at the time, but a small part of me was intrigued. Kind of excited. Like I said, I was recently divorced, and, although Rob and I still had sex on a regular basis, I was living alone and couldn't escape the feeling that something was missing from my life. So yeah, it felt kind of good when a sexy younger guy found me attractive.

A couple of days later, back at work, I finally heard the decision on my tenure bid. It was a no-go. I was floored. My ass-hat boss droned on and on about timing and budgets and enrollment trends, and then he told me that I had a couple months left to finish out the spring semester. After that, I was done.

I went through all of the stages—you know: denial, anger, acceptance, etc.—and somehow decided that the time was right to pack up and head west. It was an opportunity to start over, surrounded by red rocks. A pair of bulging biceps factored in, for sure. But I couldn't actually admit that Rick was the real motivation for my move. Not even to myself.

I did know that I needed a change and saw the tenure committee's decision as a sign. So why not, right? It's not like there was anything keeping me there. My parents had died while I was in college; Rob and I had sold our house after the divorce, and most of my things were still in storage. At the time, I was living in a tiny apartment and working like a demon at the college. Over those last few years, I had taught extra classes—all the ones that my tenured co-workers avoided—and served on so many committees, I could barely keep track of them. All in the hopes of getting tenure so I could have summers off, while sharing my love of marketing and consumer behavior with a new crop of fertile young minds every semester.

When I heard that it had all been for nothing, I was really pissed, maybe even bitter. I had sacrificed a lot for that job. I can't, in all honesty, blame my crazy workload for imploding my marriage, but it certainly hadn't helped, either. Rob and I had both been putting in tons of overtime the last few years of our seven-year marriage. He had been bucking for a partnership at the ad agency where he worked. That partnership never materialized.

So yeah, there I was, treading water and going nowhere. Falling in love with a desert community and falling in lust with one of its sexy residents wasn't what I had expected. But I did.

Before I left New England, I spent lots of time with my ex, much of it between the sheets. We didn't talk much about our future and how a few thousand miles might affect it, but Rob promised to visit me once I was settled. I hugged Suze goodbye, got in my new car, and arrived several days later in Sedona. I looked Rick up immediately. Although he had no clear recollection of who the heck I was (in his defense, nearly three months had passed; if he met fifteen tourists on an average day, well, he couldn't be blamed for failing to rec-ognize me, right?), we started seeing a lot of each other. Rick was light and breezy, fun to be around and easy to talk to.

But I wouldn't exactly describe our physical relationship as hot and heavy. After a couple of weeks of some fairly energetic sex, we quickly fell into a pattern: a couple of sleepovers a week preceded by dinner at either of our places; plus, once or twice a week, we met for lunch or dinner out, depending on Rick's crazy schedule. That was about it. Fun, sweet, and easy. Those were the hallmarks of our relationship. Nothing at all like the sizzling, sexy thrill of my first few years with Rob, but what can you do? I thought at the time that Rob had been "it" for me, and maybe I wasn't going to have another chance at a passionate love life.

Besides, I had other goals back then. Sedona was not the easiest place to start a new life. Actually, it was kind of an insular community. I made some new friends, including my landlord Coop (Edward Cooper) and the dealer of coffee (my drug of choice), barista Mo (Maureen). She and I bonded over lattes and laments about our failed relationships.

My best friend, though, was a stray tiger cat that I named Jagger. He was the coolest cat ever, with more swagger than most felines can even dream of. For the first couple of months, Jag would come and go as he pleased. He showed up to eat and sleep but spent most of the nighttime hours prowling the neighborhood. One morning, he limped in with a torn ear, looking much the worse for wear. I put my foot down and started barricading his cat door when I went to bed at night, forcing him to stay in. He didn't appear to mind his transition from alley cat to house cat, and he never strayed out of the yard after that. The day he failed to wake up from one of his long naps on our sunny patio was one of the saddest days of my life. I miss him to this day.

After taking a couple of months off to get settled, I started my own business and found it really satisfying to put my marketing skills to good use. I named my company Encore, because I offer all kinds of classes, training, and resources for midcareer types looking for a do-over, as well as those just starting out.

So there I was, trying to build a new life for myself, when my ex-husband decided to make good on his promise and pay me a visit. I think he was curious to see what I was up to and with whom, but it was immediately clear that Rob and I had unfinished business and lots of it.

The old physical attraction was still there, and, out here in the desert, our friendship was able to flourish, as well. I loved having him back in my life, and, once again, he became my biggest supporter, my best friend, and my oh-so-passionate lover. And Jag adored him, too. So I told Rick that we were not going to be hanging out any more, and Rob and I began a long-distance romance that lasted for several months.

We finally admitted to each other that there was no good reason to be anything other than totally committed, so it was his turn to pack up and move west. He bought into an ad agency out here and moved in with me, which was a good thing, as I was several months pregnant by then with our daughter.

I was skeptical at first. *I can't really be pregnant, can I?* I was nearing the age when perimenopause was just as likely the reason behind a couple of missed periods. Rob and I had talked on and off during our years together about having a child but had never gotten around to it. I had stopped even thinking of parenthood as an option.

The day Becca was born was the happiest day of my life. After nearly thirteen hours of sweaty labor, I was a mother to a wriggly, healthy bundle of joy. We named her Rebecca Sullivan Colby. I like to think that she represents the best of both me and Rob. She looks a bit more like me, with her reddish-brown hair, green eyes, and freckles, but she's got her dad's easygoing disposition and quick wit.

Once, a friend of a friend stopped me in the grocery store when Becca was about three months old. Totally sleep-deprived and running on autopilot, I was pushing Becca's stroller up and down the aisles, desperately trying to remember what had been on my grocery list, which, of course, I couldn't find. Small pieces of paper and I, we never manage to stay together very long.

"Who does she favor?" I was asked after the prerequisite *oohing* and *ahhing*.

"Oh, I think she likes both of us about the same," was my response. It wasn't until I shared the conversation with Robbie that I realized why she had looked at me so strangely.

Becca was a happy baby who grew into a happy young woman. Other than a brief period of time when she was fifteen and I was certain that aliens (horrible, pissy ones) had taken up residence in my daughter's body, I love being her mom. Robbie kept his promise of a manageable work-load, and, since I run my own business as well, one of us was usually with her during those early years. In a period of just six months, I went from living solo to having a very active family life. It was spectacular!

———————

RIGHT NOW, HOWEVER, I HAVE A SPECTACULAR MESS ON MY hands, and I am still not finished packing. One of the problems is weather, as Mother Nature can be a real bear. Unless you're going someplace with the same climate as where you're coming from, you need to pack all kinds of extra things.

Since we're travelling to Ireland, I am packing plenty of wool socks, the type of rainproof jacket I rarely if ever need in sunny Arizona, hiking boots for those "off the beaten track" trails, and lots of tanks, tees, yoga pants, and comfy stuff for long hours in the van and hanging around in our room.

Lost in thought, I jump when I hear my husband's voice. "You know, if you forget something, you can just tell me, and I'll bring it with me next week, Jaxie."

"Rob, you scared me. I hate when you do that," I complain. He crosses the room and wraps me in his arms.

"When I do what?" he asks, the picture of innocence with a devilish grin.

God, after all these years, this man still does it for me: makes my heart race, my palms sweat, weak in the knees— the whole nine yards. How can I even imagine a future without him?

"How about when I do this?" he asks, planting kisses that start at my neck and work down my arm. "Or this," he continues, taking my hand and placing it…

"Oh, gross. You two are at it again. How am I ever supposed to have a chance at a normal life with you two cavorting around like a couple of horny teenagers?" Becca plants herself firmly in the doorway and looks at us both with mock disapproval. It is true that she's grown up witnessing countless scenes like this one. She should know better, but she walked right in on us. She is obviously out of practice, as she usually calls to us from at least twenty yards away, in case anything is brewing. Her dad and I? Well, let's just say that we've never lost that lovin' feeling.

"What do you think has gone on here for the last four years, while you've been away at school, Bex?" Rob asks with a smirk. His arms still around me, he nods in my direction. "This one here? Your mom? Let me tell you, honey, she is one hot…"

"Dad, no! My ears," Becca shrieks. "I don't want to know. What happens between you two needs to stay between you two. You had to sleep together the one time, to make me, and that's it. Yuck. Anyway, I just want to ask her if she's planning on bringing any makeup remover." I just love when my two favorite people in the whole world are able to carry on a conversation like this, like I'm not even here.

Time to weigh in.

"*Her*, huh? I'm right here, my darling daughter, and yes, I just bought a new package of oil-free wipes for the trip. If you're nice to me, I'll even share them with you." I pull away from Rob. "And as for you, my darling husband, I'm going to take a rain check on whatever *this* was, okay? Right now, I need to pack." I shoo them both out of the room. First things first. A travel umbrella or something larger? Binoculars? A "real" camera? Or will I just use my phone? Decisions, decisions. Maybe more socks?

"Coop's on his way with Thai," Rob calls over his shoulder. I groan. *Crap, it's Friday*. Make that Aloha Friday. We've been getting together with our friend Coop on Friday nights since forever. We take turns hosting and alternate between a few of our favorite takeout restaurants; there's a different music theme each week. I love the tradition, and I absolutely adore Coop, but Aloha Fridays are meant to kick off a relaxing weekend with good food and great music. There is nothing relaxing about the coming weekend: twelve hours of flying, three airports, customs, etc.

I will have to limit myself to a single glass of wine tonight. I'm a bit of a lightweight when it comes to drinking, and flying is *not* my favorite pastime. Flying with a hangover would really suck.

"Okay, Rob. I'm just about done here," I assure him. And I am.

A few more pairs of socks and a shawl for my carry-on. Airplanes can be pretty chilly at times. Power cords for my phone and e-reader, and I am finished. Tomorrow morning, I will pack my makeup and toiletries and head out for a wonderful trip, during which I need to make a decision that will impact the whole rest of my life. *Yikes!*

But right now, it's time for Aloha Friday!

Becca

My mom always stresses out before she goes on a trip. The packing alone just about does her in. I mean, please. What's the worst thing that can happen? You forget something you need, like, let's just say, a phone charger. Not a tragedy, people. You pick up a spare at the airport or any number of shops spread across the whole world. If you were going on an African safari and forgot your phone charger, I guess that would be a different situation. But then, you probably wouldn't get cell coverage anyway, so who cares about a missing charger? Anyway, I have bigger issues to deal with today. Like, oh, I don't know, *my life*?

My mom and I are going on a tour of Ireland to celebrate my recent college graduation, and, in about a week and a half, my dad will be joining us. We'll head up to Northern Ireland for a few days and then fly back here to Sedona. So I have definite plans for the next few weeks.

Once we return home, I'll divide my waking hours between working for my mom, my dad, and my Aunt Mo.

Hopefully fit in some time to shop and read. Get a couple of pedis and drink gallons of iced coffee. That will take me right through the summer. Yeah, and one more thing: I have a class to make up. Well, complete, actually.

I *know* I said I graduated, but, technically…? I dropped the ball during the last semester, and my final paper, well, I never turned it in. I threw myself on the mercy of the professor. Thankfully, I'm not usually one for excuses and she knew that. So when I said, "I blew it. I'm sorry," she was cool. I could have flunked the course, but she gave me an incomplete. As long as I turn in the paper by mid-July, she'll adjust the grade at that time.

But I haven't told my folks yet. A couple weeks back, when they called my name at commencement and I marched up to get my diploma, I received the same empty envelope that all my classmates did. The only difference? Everyone else received real diplomas in the mail last week.

My mom has been hounding me and keeps telling me to call the school and find out where mine is, and I can't keep putting her off. She's been real distracted lately, and there's definitely something going on with her and Dad. They're having some sort of disagreement, and they're doing their best to keep it from me. I am going to have to figure out a time to tell her during the trip. I know she'll flip out, so I may have to wait until she's all mellow after a day of sight-seeing and a couple glasses of wine. As soon as we get back to Sedona, I'll get to work on the darn paper. So it's going to be a super busy summer. After that, things are not so clear.

I plan to go to grad school back in Boston, at the same school where I've been doing my undergraduate degree in psychology. I love the university, love Boston, and I'm excited about the idea of going back there. To the city; not back to school. I've been thinking I should probably take a year or two off. Get out there in the real world before hitting the books for a few more long years. My academic advisor suggested it months ago, and my parents did, too.

I'm toying with the idea of holding off, but I keep coming back to the same old question. *What the hell am I supposed to do, if I'm not in school?* Who is Becca, if she's not a full-time student? It's part of who I am. Hell, it *is* who I am. I've always been a good student, but I've had to work hard to get the grades that put me on the honor roll and the Dean's List.

One semester, I got the opportunity to intern at a teen center. What a great experience *that* was. I dished out dating advice and condoms like a champ. I think I really connected with those kids. During my senior year, my classmates started to talk about internships and full-time career type jobs. We were encouraged to draft cover letters, practice our interviewing skills, and build our "network." I was freaking out. My mom teaches people how to do all that, so I know what it entails, but still. The whole process was overwhelming and the thought of finishing college felt scary. Maybe that's why I blew off the paper.

And it's a lot harder to work on all of those things if you haven't narrowed down where you plan to live. And I haven't. Don't get me wrong, I love Sedona. It's beautiful and friendly and familiar. But I keep telling myself that it's time to spread my wings and fly a little. Boston is a great place to live. It seems like there are lots of opportunities, and I've gotten used to the snow and the cold after four years. I can see myself moving there, but what will I do?

I can work in an office doing something or other, or work in retail, I guess, like some of my classmates. But those jobs don't pay very well, and Boston is an expensive place to live. I would end up sharing a tiny walk-up with two or three roommates and barely breaking even.

I can live for free, if I move back home, I guess, and I know that I can find work. Ever since I was fourteen, I've spent breaks and weekends working in my mom's consulting business or my dad's advertising agency or my Aunt Mo's café. But with graduation looming, I decided to apply to grad school and got accepted for this fall. Seemed like a good idea at first, but I am starting to have second thoughts.

If I back out now, I'll probably lose my deposit, and I don't know if they would hold a seat for me for next semester or next year. I've committed to being a resident advisor for the upcoming academic year, as well. Free room and board and a stipend that will keep me in lattes and Netflix, but very little else.

Damn. The decision is really starting to weigh on me. I am looking forward to a few relaxing weeks in Ireland. I need to clear my head and finally decide what I want to do with my life. Take in the sights, and catch up on my sleep. And come clean with my mom. So yeah, worrying about packing an extra pair of socks or a spare charger? Not sweating that.

If you enjoyed this preview of *Driving on the Left*, it is available in print and kindle versions. Check it out here: www.GailOlmsted.com

Acknowledgements

I have to thank my early readers for volunteering (or agreeing) to give their time and provide valuable feedback to me as I was writing my first novel: Laurie Cain, Louise Corcoran, Karen Jordan, Eve Kinne, Robin Lee, Diane Sabato, and Barbara Wurtzel: thank you ladies for your insight, friendship and support!

Also, I need to thank Diane Sabato for joining me on a fun and very valuable fact-finding visit to Sedona, my second trip there! To Elke Wardell, and to my nephew Chris Ward—thank you for letting me get into your heads and allowing me insights to your Gen X lives.

Made in the USA
Las Vegas, NV
09 January 2025

16117610R00142